THE MEN AND
WOMEN, THE HOURS AND
MINUTES, THE FEARS, LOVES, CRIES,
SHOTS, AND TURMOIL OF
THE BATTLE OF LEXINGTON
brought to life by America's most
powerful historical novelist,
HOWARD FAST,
author of CITIZEN TOM PAINE
and
SPARTACUS.

---

**APRIL MORNING**
A novel about one of the most glorious
days in American history, a book for
everyone—everywhere!

# April Morning

## by Howard Fast

BANTAM BOOKS

TORONTO • NEW YORK • LONDON • SYDNEY • AUCKLAND

RL 5, IL age 12 and up

APRIL MORNING

*A Bantam Book / published by arrangement with
Crown Publishers, Inc.*

*PRINTING HISTORY*
Crown edition published April 1961
2nd printing ............ April 1961    3rd printing ............ June 1961
4th printing .................... August 1961
*Bantam edition / April 1962
28 printings through August 1981*

ISBN 0–553–20593–5

*Published simultaneously in the United States and Canada*

---

*Bantam Books are published by Bantam Books, Inc. Its trade-
mark, consisting of the words "Bantam Books" and the por-
trayal of a rooster, is Registered in U.S. Patent and Trademark
Office and in other countries. Marca Registrada. Bantam
Books, Inc., 666 Fifth Avenue, New York, New York 10103.*

---

PRINTED IN THE UNITED STATES OF AMERICA

37  36  35  34  33  32

*Since in one way or another a part of
each of you is in this book, it is properly yours.
Thereby, for Rachel, Jonathan, Barry, Judy,
Norman, Jennifer, Melissa, and Timothy.*

# *The Afternoon*

When I turned back to the house, my father called after me and asked me did I figure that I was finished. "I figure so," I said, and then my father said, in that way he has of saying something that cuts you down to half of your size or less:

"Slow to start and quick to finish."

He said it plain and quiet, but it was of a piece and it reminded me that I couldn't think of a time when he had said something pleasing or gentle with love or concern; and I replied to him, but not aloud—for which I didn't have the guts at all— "If just once in all my born days you'd say a good thing to me, then maybe I'd show good to you, and be able to do what you want me to do, and maybe read your mind or your soul." But aloud I said nothing, just began to walk toward the house, and his voice coiled after me like a whip around my ankle:

"Adam!"

"Yes, sir."

"I'll have you talk to me face to face, not into the air with your back to me."

"Yes, sir," I said, turning around.

"Draw your mother's evening water and bring it to her. Wasted steps are like wasted thoughts, just as empty and just as ignorant."

"Yes, Father," I said, and I went to the house and picked up the yoke and walked with it to the well. The sun was cutting. That's the time of the day when the wind stops, and the air is so sweet you can taste it and suck it.

3

But that afternoon, the time of the day made me think about death, and I saw a chicken hawk in flight and waited for someone somewhere to send a load of bird shot after it; but no one did. I thought of death and was full of fear, and I just wanted to sit down somewhere and put my face in my hands and give in to the terrible frightened feeling I had; but I didn't. I have all kinds of strange thoughts and feelings of that sort, and I guess I never talked to anyone about them, except perhaps a little to Granny, because I didn't really believe that anyone in the world ever had just the same kind of thoughts.

When I drew the water from the well, I said the spell to take the curse off water, "Holy ghost and holy hell, get thee out of the mossy well." My father once heard me say that spell, and he took me into the barn and gave me seven with the birch rod. He hated spells and said they were worse than an instrument of the devil; they were an instrument of ignorance. And I was foolish enough to answer back that if he was so sure about all kinds of superstition, why did he birch me seven times, not eight or six? That was the way it was in the whole town. When you got the rod taken to you, you got it seven times.

I should have known enough to keep my mouth shut, because he replied that he was gratified to be enlightened and laid onto me ten times more, and then wanted to know whether I deemed seventeen to be a superstitious number?

So now I said the spell quietly, just moving my lips; a spell has no meaning if you only think it to yourself and never voice it. But quiet or not, my brother Levi, who is eleven years old, has cat's eyes. He popped up and demanded a drink from the bucket.

4

"Draw your own water," I told him.

"Don't be high and mighty. I seen you saying the spell. How would you like for me to tell Father that I seen you saying the spell?"

"You're a little bastard," I told him.

"Sure, and what did you just call your mother?"

"All right. Take your drink and leave me be. Why don't you stay out of my sight. I'd be happy to God if only you'd stay out of my sight."

I took a drink too. The water is always best, cold and crackling, when you first draw it.

When I came into the house, Mother was frying donkers, and the kitchen was full of the smell. You save a week's meat leftovers to make donkers, and then it's chopped together with bread and apples and raisins and savory spices, and fried and served up with boiled pudding. I don't know of anything better. When my mother saw me come in with the yoke, she took the water off and smiled her gratitude.

"You're a good boy, Adam," she said.

I didn't tell her that it wasn't my idea. I needed for someone to think something good about me, and I didn't want to disturb her thinking. When I ate some of the raw meatstuff, she slapped my hand. When I sat down, she said:

"Are you going to stay here and fill my head with your nonsense?"

"What nonsense? I haven't said a word."

"That's just it, Adam. You sit there with that look in your eyes, and just as plain as daylight I can see what kind of silly dream you're contemplating. When I was your age, if a boy had an hour between the chores and mealtime, he spent it with profit reading the Holy Writ. Granny told me how your father—just about your age it was—set him-

5

self a disciplined period to memorize three verses of Lamentations every evening."

"Lamentations?"

"And he did."

"Well, good heavens, what on earth did he want to memorize the verses of Lamentations every evening for?"

"To profit himself. And let me tell you this, Adam," she said. "I don't hold with the narrow views of some, but it seems to me that an expression like *good heavens* is precious close to swearing. It seems to me that the King's English is abundant enough to express every necessary shade of feeling and impatience without resorting to words that have sincere meaning when used properly. Have you been fighting with your brother again?"

"Now what gave you that idea?" I didn't wait for her to tell me, but got up and began to stalk out the way I had come. She had to know where I was going.

"Just to find Granny."

"She's upstairs."

I went upstairs, and Granny was in her room making thread. When I entered, she blinked at me and said, "I see less and less. Old age is pity enough, but when the eyesight goes, the good Lord is laying a heavy burden on my poor shoulders."

"Well, Granny," I replied, "I don't think your eyesight is going. It's just getting dark in here because the twilight has come down."

"Is that so, Adam?"

"Sure enough."

"Well, then, I've spun sufficiently," she declared. "Sit down, Adam. Do you want some sweets?"

I sat down on her old milking stool, which she

had decorated with paint and turned into one of the prettiest things in the house, and reminded her that there was a widely held opinion to the effect that sweets before mealtime spoil an appetite.

"Oh?" she said. "I'm sure we'd all be rich if I could devise something to spoil your appetite, Adam." Then she went to the cupboard and got out the cotton kerchief that she always wrapped the maple sugar in, and she broke off a piece for each of us. I ate it slowly and appreciatively, and asked her whether it was true about my father, and Lamentations.

"It's true."

"Well, what for? I mean, what was his purpose?"

"To profit himself."

"That's what Mother said, but I'll be damned if I can see the profit in it."

"You will be damned, Adam, if you go on with such talk." I shrugged. "And don't act as if you don't care."

"I think we keep saying things that we don't really mean at all, Granny."

"Do we? And what sort of things, Adam?"

"Like being damned. Do you believe in God, Granny?"

"What a question!" She snorted with great indignation. "In all my born days, Adam Cooper, I have never seen a boy like yourself for asking questions!"

"Well, do you?"

"Of course I do."

"Well, I don't know—"

"Adam Cooper, you are not going to start in again with all that silly nonsense of yours, are you?"

"Just one thing—just answer me one thing,

Granny, that's all I'm asking. I just want you to answer me one thing. What is it that they're always taking it out on me for whatever I say, like there's nothing in the world I can do right and everything I do is all wrong?"

"My goodness, the things you say, Adam!"

"Well, look at it this way, Granny. You believe in God, don't you?"

"Enough of that."

"If you believe in God, then God gave a person brains, didn't he?"

"Of course."

"But just as soon as you begin to use the brains God gave you, you're being sinful."

"That's just the sort of foolish thing you say, Adam, that's so provoking."

"Well, just take Isaiah Peterkin, for example."

"Oh, no," she said, her eyes narrowing, "I am not going to be trapped into the Isaiah Peterkin thing. It just happens that I was gathering blueberries the other day, and there you were down in the gully with Ruth Simmons, instructing her about Isaiah Peterkin, and I overheard enough—"

"Did you see us, Granny?"

"I didn't have to see you. As if I wouldn't know that Cooper voice of yours anywhere!"

I sighed with relief, and told her that even if I had gone into it a little with Ruth Simmons, that didn't make it any less a fact.

"It just seems to me, Adam," Granny said, "that shaking a body loose from her faith is about the most sinful thing you could do."

"Granny, I wasn't shaking anybody loose from anybody's faith. I'd like you to tell me how old Isaiah can be as mean and wicked and two-faced as he is, and be a deacon in the church and be looked up to as a real fine God-fearing man. I mean, he can get away with anything, just so long as he says the right words about religion."

"It's not for you to judge Isaiah Peterkin."

"I wasn't judging him," I protested. "Everyone knows how rich and mean he is. So how could I be judging him? Anyway, in Boston when we were there a fortnight past, there was a man talking right on the Common, and he said that the highest good was to doubt. Just like that, in those very words."

"I never heard such nonsense. If he said that, he was nobody worth quoting."

"He was a Committeeman, Granny."

"I don't believe a word of it."

"Cross my heart, Granny."

"Don't you dare cross your heart to me," she snapped, "just like you was Roman or some other heathen sect, and don't think that because I'm old and rheumatic and grateful for foolish company that you can say anything you please in front of me. You can't cozen me with a pretense at stupidity, not in one thousand years. You're a spiteful boy, and that's why your father loses patience with you."

"He doesn't lose patience, Granny. He doesn't have any patience to begin with."

"There!"

"And this was a Committeeman," I said.

"So. Well, just tell me this—was he a Sam Adams Committeeman?"

I admitted that he was most likely a Sam Adams Committeeman, and she shrugged her shoulders and said there wasn't anything else a body could expect, seeing that Sam Adams was an atheist and so were all of his cronies. Granny had a good mind, and I guess that was one of the reasons why I enjoyed provoking her. The other reason was that she would stand for being provoked, and practically no one else would. "Now if he had said, Adam," she went on, "that one of the paths to good was a certain amount of doubt and common sense, there might be some reason to his thoughts. Then he would have been sensible. But doubt is a negative thing and good is a positive thing, and anyone who says that both are the same thing is simply a fool, and there you are."

"That's it exactly, Granny. When you disagree with someone, you straight out and call them a fool. But when I disagree, I get my ears pinned back."

"I'm older than you, Adam, by a year or two."

"You said yourself that age doesn't teach most folks a blessed thing."

"Don't tell me what I said. If you propose to remain as narrow and opinionated as you are now all the years of your life—well, that's your choice. *Most* folks are one thing. I should hope that my grandson would be something else."

At that moment, Mother called from below that supper was ready, and I gave Granny my arm and helped her down the stairs. Her rheumatism was getting worse and worse. As we went down the staircase, myself a little in front of her because the staircase was so narrow, she said to me:

"Don't ever talk *most* to me, Adam. *Most* folks are not Coopers, and *most* folks do not live in this village or in this county either. *Most* folks are not dissenters, and *most* folks would just as soon find a chain to put around their necks, considering one wasn't there already. Coopers have been teachers and pastors and free yeomen farmers and ship captains and merchants for a hundred and fifty years on this soil, and I don't recall one of them who couldn't write a sermon and deliver it too, if the need ever arose."

"Well, maybe you're leaning on the first one, Granny," I said.

On Weekdays, we ate our meals in the kitchen. On the Sabbath, we ate dinner in the dining room, and Mother set the table with china and silver. We weren't rich, but Granny's mother had been rich enough for china and silver. On weekdays, we ate with plainware.

Although there were only five of us in the immediate family, our table was always set with places for six, Mother at one end, Father at the other, Granny facing the two boys. The empty chair was next to Granny. My father claimed that the empty chair was, as he put it, a manifesto of hospitality, an invitation to anyone who crossed our threshold at mealtime; and I must admit that many a guest sat there, knowing that the welcome was ready at the Coopers', the food good and the cooking beyond compare. But my father's real purpose was an audience, and if possible an argument. There wasn't anyone in his own family whom he considered really worth arguing with, and as far as plain discourse was concerned, although we were a disciplined and trained audience, he could never be wholly sure that we were listening, and if listening, comprehending.

My own opinion was that Granny could win hands down in any argument, but she would not argue with her son in front of his own children. She also felt that one of her sex tended to be unlady-like and pushy when she ventured on the finer points of the divine, ordinary, and inherent rights of man—which was mainly the subject.

Tonight, however, we had no guest at the

beginning of the meal, and the five of us sat down and four of us bent our heads while Father said grace. He didn't hold with bending his head, at grace or any other time, and when Granny once raised this point with him, he replied that one of the many differences between ourselves and Papists and High Church people—who were a shade worse than Papists—was that whereas the latter two sects cringed and groveled before the clay and plaster images they worshiped, we stood face to face with our God, as befitting what He had created in His own image. Granny said that there was possibly some difference between cringing and groveling and a polite bending of the head from the neck, but Father wasn't moved. The difference was quantitative, and therefore only a matter of degree. To him it was a principle. In two minutes, my father could lead any argument or discussion around to being a principle.

So he said grace glaring across the table at the imaginary point where he placed God, and I always felt that God had the worst of it. My father couldn't just begin a meal with something direct and ordinary, like "Thank Thee, O Lord, for Thy daily bread and the fruit of the harvest." Oh, no—no, he had to embellish it. If there was no guest at the meal, God was always present, and tonight my father said sternly:

"We thank thee, O Lord, for the bread we eat, but we are also conscious of seed we have planted, of the hands that guided the plow and the back bent in toil. The ground is dry as dust, and I will take the liberty of asking for a little rain. I know that Thou givest with one hand and Thou takest away with the other, but sometimes it seems to me to go beyond the bounds of reason. Amen!"

Then he turned to his soup. Granny lifted her

head and stared at him, and finally said, "Moses?"

"Yes, Mother?"

She sighed, and we all began to eat.

"Yes, Mother?"

"Nothing," Granny said. "Nothing at all."

"Whatever is on your mind, Mother, I would appreciate your coming out with it and saying it."

"Eat your soup, Moses," she sighed.

He was inordinately fond of soup, and during the soup he left conversation to the women and children. I did not have much to say to Levi, being occupied with my own thoughts, some of them about Ruth Simmons and also some thoughts about going to sea. If you had respectable kin in Boston, it was generally understood that one of the younger sons would go to sea and learn the trade, since there was no better way to end up with a fine house and a wife in silks and laces, and good, imported furniture as well as some standing in the community. I was not a younger son, but one day in Boston, Captain Ishmael Jamison, my uncle on my mother's side, had felt my muscles, asked me a number of questions, and finished by wondering how I would like to sign on with him as bottom junior on a voyage to the Indies. I was remembering this, contemplating it, and speculating on whether there weren't more interesting girls in the world than Ruth Simmons, whom I had seen at least every day of my life. I also kept in back of my mind a picture of my father's rage if I came out with so much as a hint about going to sea.

At the same time, Mother and Granny talked about the quilt competition. There were those in the village who held that any sort of competition was vain and sinful, and no better than another form of pride. Granny put out that it was pure nonsense that the acknowledgment that one person did something better than another was sinful. She made the best and most colorful quilts in town, and had been quietly pumping for a competition for years.

"It's not for the sake of a prize or money," Granny said. "I do suppose that if there was something to be won or gained, it might be likened to a form of gambling."

"What's this about gambling?" my father demanded. He had finished his soup.

"If Sarah Livingston could win, not likely, since she can't sew three stitches straight, we'd have the contest, she being married to the elder, be sure of that," Mother said.

"Gambling?"

"Eat your supper," Granny told Father. "What is a turkey shoot but gambling and sin? What is the lottery they hold each year in Boston?—and don't tell me that only High Church buys the tickets."

"Did I say that?"

I helped Mother take the empty dishes off and bring on the platters of meat cakes and potatoes and parsnips and boiled pudding.

"You were about to, Moses."

"What is all this talk about gambling?"

"It's woman talk. Pass me your plate."

It did me good to see Granny treating my father as if he was half grown. She has an instinct about when he is preparing to bear down on me, and she figured that a little humility would lessen the blows. But he also saw where the wind was blowing and didn't waste another minute. No sooner had he swallowed his first mouthful of donker than he said to me:

"How big are you, Adam?"

"Tall?"

"Do you know other ways of being big?"

I could have managed a clever answer to that one, but I saw the glint in his eyes and decided to accept the sameness of big and tall and not promote an argument. It has always been a wonder to me that anyone could work up a rancor toward anything while eating my mother's cooking, but when something was on Father's mind, it couldn't wait.

"No, sir," I agreed.

"Then what is your height, Adam?"

My mother knew that my father was most ominous when he indulged in innocent and obvious questions, and she pressed him to take more boiled pudding. He cut the ground from under her by accepting another helping, but Granny said:

"Whatever this is, Moses, it can wait until the meal is over. Adam won't be any taller then than he is right now."

Levi was too silent and expectant. I began to get the drift of things.

"Let me decide that," Father said, "and suppose you answer the question, Adam." He went on with the boiled pudding, and I decided that if we could get this all out while we were eating it would be less painful to everyone. I told him, very seriously, that I stood somewhere between twenty-three and twenty-four hands, most likely closer to twenty-four, since I was at least two inches taller than Ebenezer Coult, who claimed he just topped twenty-three.

"Tall as a man," my father nodded.

"Some men," I agreed, and did not think it wise to add that I was taller than most.

"And strong as a man. Then one would think that a man's mind would go along with all that. Don't you think so, Adam?"

"Yes, sir. I mean it appears to make sense."

"Only appears so, Adam?" Father asked softly.

"Oh, have some donkers," Granny said. "All this is going to interfere with your digestion. You know that, Moses."

"I asked Adam a question."

"Yes, sir," I nodded.

"How long is a man supposed to watch his son and wonder?"

"I don't know, sir."

"Do you expect me to take you out and birch you?"

"No, sir. I'm a little large for that," I whispered. "It wouldn't be dignified. It wouldn't do me any good either. It would get around."

"I'm not sparing you for the sake of your reputation among your cronies."

I nodded. "I know that, sir."

"Just as you know why I am angry?"

"Yes, sir. Levi couldn't keep his mouth shut."

My father accepted a donker from Granny and took a large bite of the boiled pudding, and I knew that the worst was over and that for the moment I was saved. He had put punishment aside for the moment and would employ reason as his weapon. I don't know which made me feel worse, and the only compensation was some speculation on what I would do to Levi. My father must have read my mind, because he said:

"I don't want you to turn this on Levi, Adam. He did what was right. Don't you agree with me?"

I nodded, not trusting myself to look at Levi; and my father, now enjoying his food and digestion and the soft whip hand he had established over me, continued:

"Why am I angry, Adam? Is it because you repeated some foolish childish doggerel when you drew the water from the well? Hardly. I hate and despise superstition, not because it is blasphemous but because it is a display of ignorance." He let the food go as he warmed up to this; my father was a fine talker, and I guess he derived more pure pleasure from it than from any other habit. "We are plain people," he continued, "not poor—for we are blessed with more than a necessary share of the world's goods, and we have a good house with good furniture and good food on our table, for which we thank the Lord in His mercy—but plain and thrifty people. Yet we, your mother, myself, my father, and my grandfather—we have always prided ourselves that we are in a sense the people of the Book. My brothers and I were raised, and I make every effort to raise my own children, not as blackguards and loafers, not as soldiers or tavern sots, but as thoughtful and reasoning creatures, men who honor the written word, who respect intelligent writing, and who, like the ancient philosophers, look upon argumentation and disputation as avenues toward the deepest truth. I am a farmer who tills the soil to earn his daily bread, but there are three hundred and odd books in this house, well thumbed, well read. Nor are my neighbors unlike me. This is why, Adam, we are what we are. We came to this land in the beginning because savagery and superstition were an abomination to us, and in the midst of a new savagery, we planted our own seed of culture and civilization. Do you understand me?" he finished.

"Well, he may but I don't," Granny put in decisively, and I could see that she had decided to take the bit in her teeth. "To make a fuss like that over the foolishness of a fifteen-year-old just passes my understanding, it does. Why, believe me, I never did see a man to sit at his own supper table and be faced with the kind of food Sarah Cooper puts down in front of you, Moses Cooper, and be that ill-tempered."

"Now, please, Mother—"

"Don't stop me in the middle of a sentence, Moses Cooper."

"I didn't stop you in the middle of a sentence."

"Not to mention pride," Granny went on. "It goeth before a fall, or doesn't it? And if that wasn't the most prideful statement I ever listened to, then I don't know what was. A spell may be un-Christian and ignorant, but let me remind you what the Testament says about pride—"

"I know what the Testament says about pride, Mother."

We were interrupted at that point, or I don't know where it would have gone on to. My mother was nervous and upset over the whole thing; Levi was sunk in gloom, brooding on what I might do to him later, and very disturbed that Granny had gone after Father the way she had; but I was enjoying it the way you enjoy running on the edge of a high stone cliff. It's exhilarating while it lasts. It finished because Joseph Simmons, our neighbor and kin, came in and gave his greetings, and said that he would just sit down in the empty chair and watch us while we finished our evening bread.

But he wouldn't have a thing to eat. A mouthful would be too much, as he had just finished his own supper. But then he saw that we were having donkers, and he admitted that he might try one, he was so inordinately fond of them, and since it didn't go alone, he'd have a mouthful of boiled pudding on the plate. Mother gave him hot meat from the fire, and it was a pleasure to see his face when he took the first bite. He was a big, heavy-set

man, and I never saw anyone to match him for
straightforward pleasure in food.

"Goody Cooper," he said to my mother, "I don't
recollect a more delicious meat than your donkers.
But neither do I recollect any home but yours
where they're favored."

"They're not proper English food," said Mother. "They're Dutch food."

"Now what do you know!"

"You see, my grandfather Isaac, he was in the
coasting trade."

"I've heard about your grandfather Isaac,
indeed," said Mr. Simmons. Unlike my father, he
did not have to stop eating to talk; he did both at
once. He said it respectfully, but nevertheless it
gave my mother a twinge. She pretends not to
know how many have heard and gossiped about her
grandfather Isaac, who kept one wife and family
in Boston and another wife and family in Philadelphia, but the knowledge was widespread. The
fact that the Philadelphia wife was one half
Shawnee Indian and had never been baptized—
as the story went—gave the gossip an added fillip.
While her grandfather Isaac was alive, she
couldn't bear to speak of him or listen to him being spoken of; but when he died and left her two
hundred sovereigns, Father said that his sinfulness
took a back seat to his generosity and thoughtful-
ness. In addition, a sea captain was never judged
by the same standards we used to measure a
landsman.

"Of course." Mother nodded. "Well, one day at
sea, his cook died of the ague, and he put into
New York harbor and engaged a Holland cook,
and after that he never could sail with anything
but a Holland cook, and he got a taste for Dutch

cooking in his own home. It was the Holland cook taught Grandmother Zipporah things like donkers, and I got the recipes from her."

"One more, Cousin Simmons," Granny said. He was a second cousin on the Cooper side.

He said he didn't have the strength or the lasting power for another meat cake, but Mother knew as well as I did that he was saving himself for a piece of her pie. He explained that he had come by to walk with my father to the extraordinary Committee meeting they were holding tonight. Two weeks before this, the Committee had appointed him to write a statement on the rights of man, to which they would all put their names, and which would be posted in Boston. In my opinion, which nobody asked, Joseph Simmons was a poor choice. He was a nice enough man, but when it came to the fine points of disputation, he simply wasn't there. He had been working on the draft of his statement for two weeks, and most likely he'd work on it two weeks more. It would have been more natural for the Committee to select my father or Deacon Loring or Mr. Harrington for the task, but my father was a Company Captain and all sorts of positions and titles had been handed out to the others. That left Cousin Simmons for the statement.

He took his draft out of his pocket now, and then told Father he had been waiting for an opportunity to have his considered opinion.

"Go ahead and read it, Joseph," Father said.

Cousin Simmons cleared his throat and read, "We, the undersigned, holding to the positive and practical position that the rights of men are derived from Almighty God and sealed by His holy hand and will—"

He was watching Father's face, and his voice died away. "Well, Moses?" he said tentatively.

"Go ahead and read."

Granny and Mother were dishing the pie and putting the plates on the table. Cousin Simmons couldn't resist tasting it.

"Go on and read, I said."

"Well, what's the use of reading? Why don't you come out and say what's on your mind? I can't go on reading with your face all screwed up in disagreement."

Granny said, "I can't see what's to disagree with when you've hardly begun."

"I wasn't disagreeing," Father said. "I was just thinking that when you leave church, theology won't hold water. I don't argue against a man's religion. And I don't want him to dispute me with his religion."

"For heaven's sake," Granny said, "Cousin Simmons no more than read the preamble."

"Just as important as any of the rest of it."

"And how have I been disputing you with religion, Moses? I'd like you to make that plain."

"Rights derived from God! That's no argument—that's a swamp. You'll get neck-deep in that. Fat George doesn't blow his nose without it's a God-given right, clear and simple. Why, I think the meanest, lowest thing about these wars they fight in Europe is the way both parties to the affair have God marching shoulder to shoulder with them."

"Now if that isn't blasphemous, I don't know what is!" Granny snapped.

"Nothing of the kind! I respect my Maker, I don't invoke Him. We wouldn't have the Committee, or need it either, if God just handed out His

rights left and right. When God made man, He
gave him a mind to consider with and two hands to
set things right."

"I was just putting it in a manner of speaking,"
Simmons protested.

"We can't afford to put things in a manner of
speaking, Joseph. We have got to set out our line
clear and proper, and prove it all the way. Oh
yes, the pastor will hold that our rights derive from
God. That's his business. He has to. But you and
me, we know well enough that it was only because of a lot of stiff-necked people like ourselves
that we have got a knowledge of rights. You consider my Uncle Cyrus in the rum trade. He says
he'll die and see his ship and fortune sunk before
he hands his trade over to the British. He has the
right to trade with the islands because he backs up
that right with his life. Same way, I hold this house
of mine a castle inviolate—but that's pure boasting
unless the Committee backs me up. Do you see?"

But Cousin Simmons was slow to see, and they
went on discussing it over the pie and afterwards
as they were preparing to leave the house. I
stopped my father in the kitchen as they were
leaving, and I said to him:

"I want to go with you to the meeting, Father."

"Oh?"

"I know that the Committee made a rule about
sixteen years before a man enters—"

"Are you a man now, Adam?"

"I'm tall and strong and only nine months
away from my sixteenth birthday."

"The proof of a man is the will to work and
the ability to use his mind and his judgment. Can
you offer that proof, Adam?"

I stared at him in silence.

"Talk to me when you can, Adam."

Then they both left.

Granny said that there was more pure non-sense connected with a Committee meeting than a body could bear, and she didn't see why I would want to waste the evening hours there. My mother put her arm around my shoulders.

"Why does he hate me so?" I asked them.

"Hate you?" Mother said. "Adam, he loves you. You're his son."

"Then I got love and hate mixed up."

"What a way to talk!"

"How do you expect me to talk? Has he ever said a kind word to me? He chops at me like I was an old, dry pine for him to temper his ax on. Whatever I do, it's not right, and no matter how I do it, he finds fault."

"That's just his way."

"Is it? Well, it's not my way to like it."

Granny said gently, "Oh, Adam, Adam, what a fuss to make over a cantankerous man who's enamored with the sound of his own voice! Moses Cooper is your father and I suppose he can't ever be anything else but that to you, but to old Goody Cooper here, he's just a son, just the same as you are, and he's never been any different but the way he is now, pigheaded and full of his own notions. Do you think poor Cousin Simmons could ever have written that statement to suit Moses Cooper? No, sir. Cousin Simmons might be the nicest and most delicate writer in all the county, but that wouldn't satisfy Moses Cooper. He'd find fault."

"All I ever asked from him is one kind word. Just so he'd look at me once as if I wasn't dirt scraped out of the barnyard."

"He just expects more than a soul can deliver," Granny said.

I pulled away from Mother and started toward the door.

"Where are you going, Adam?"

"Out."

"Adam, don't press it. Don't go over to the church. If your father sees you there after he ordered you not to come, he'll be very angry."

"He's always angry. Anyway, I'm not going to bother their damned Committee—"

"Adam!"

I stalked out to the yard, and there was Levi crouching in the shadows. It was dark now.

"Adam?"

"Go to hell, you little rat," I told him.

"You going to lick me, Adam?"

"Did I ever lick you?"

"No. But there's always a first time, Adam."

"There will be if you don't stay out of my sight."

## The Evening

I have told more or less what happened in the afternoon, through the meal-time—and I suppose it is for the most part what happened to me, or what I heard or what I saw. As far as the afternoon is concerned, I don't think that it makes too much difference, because allowing for our family's characteristics, everyone else in the village was eating their supper at about the same time. It is true that most of them were having chicken or salt pork, but we can accept the fact that in half of the homes, pie was taken for dessert, and you could safely say that three-quarters of them had boiled pudding. There was a sharp dividing line in our town between those women who cooked their boiled pudding in the old-fashioned English way, out of fine wheat flour and suet. The other half used ground yellow maize. We had stopped using flour after my father somehow connected English pudding with a conciliative point of view— something which Mother's sewing circle regarded as the highest achievement of logic during the past year; and you may believe that we saw some high moments of logic in our village. If it had been up to Granny, she never would have budged an inch, but Mother gave in, partly because deep down under everything, she admired Father's gift for argumentation. I once heard her state that she was quite proud of the fact that while Father could have argued any girl in New England into being his wife, he had chosen her to persuade. But there was also the fact that most of Mother's friends had already switched to maize. You would hardly believe this, but the maize-flour controversy reached such a pitch of philosophical excitement that there were a few days when half the women in the village just stopped talking to the other half. If the Reverend hadn't taken the situation in hand and preached one of his hottest sermons on the relationship of the fruits of the earth to plain, downright human foolishness, I don't know where it would have all ended.

But however the boiled pudding was made, it was eaten widely that night, as on most nights, and afterwards the men trooped over to the church for the Committee meeting. While I wasn't at the meeting, it seems to me that I ought to report something of what went on there. I was in bed when Father came home later that night, and heard him give Mother and Granny a full report, but to have things in proper sequence, I will deal with that now, before I tell what happened to me during the evening.

The meeting was called to order by Samuel Hodley, after which Jeremiah Phitts gave the financial report. That went its usual course, ending up with a balance of twelve shillings, sixpence. An assessment of threepence on all present was moved and voted. My father reported that a considerable number deferred payment.

Samuel Hodley took the floor again and gave the results of the weapons count for the village and surrounding area. It came to one hundred and sixteen assorted pieces. As near as my father could remember, it broke down somewhat in this fashion: there were seven close-bore guns with rifled barrels, a small number, but rifles are expensive instruments and the very devil to load. There were some sixty-odd smoothbore guns, of which about ten were old-fashioned firelocks. Among these sixty were fourteen British army guns, which had traveled to us—that is, they belonged to the Committee—a nice way of saying that they were stolen. There were five dragoon pistols, but these were the kind that a family bought to show off on the mantel in the sitting room, and it was questionable whether they would work. All the rest were fowling guns for pepper and salt shot.

Hodley wanted a central shot and powder depot organized in the village, because he had read somewhere that any place under siege should have an ammunition depot; but since we were not under siege and most likely never would be, his point was voted down.

Then Clarence Pinckney brought up his pet notion about drilling, but April was the wrong month to ask hard-working farmers to come out into the sunshine and drill, so the matter was put off for a fortnight. Cousin Simmons gave a progress report on the statement he had in preparation, and then the Reverend said a few words on tyranny, taxes, the moral condition of the High Church, the proper place of Oliver Cromwell in history as opposed to his current slanderers and detractors—and finished by paraphrasing the first two books of Maccabees.

Some of the more orthodox held that it was presumptuous of the Reverend to push Maccabees the way he did, since those books were more properly apocryphal than divine, but the Reverend would have none of such criticism. We were the brothers of Simon, he said, and if God put such a weapon as Maccabees I and II into his hand, he would strike with the weapon or shame the gift of the Almighty. I don't remember a case where the Reverend got the worst of that kind of an argument.

Next, they took up the discussion of a newspaper. No one really believed that a community as small as ours could actually support a newspaper, nor did anyone ever really sit down with it and try to figure out where the capital for beginning the venture would be found, the round sum of money needed for the printing press, the type faces, the ink and the newsprint. Instead, the discussion always turned into a hot debate between the pro-Samuel Adams radicals and the anti-Samuel Adams egalitarians, since it was Adams who again and again stated that a newspaper must be the connecting link between the Committees and the people. As far as our village was concerned, within a few hours after a Committee meeting was finished, every soul in the place knew every word that had been spoken—so I failed to see Mr. Adams' point.

But such a discussion did provide the philosophical content without which no Committee meeting was complete, and it gave my father, who had always dreamed of himself as a newspaper editor whose flaming words would arouse thousands to action, an opportunity to plunge into the fray. I never could understand whether he enjoyed the points Samuel Adams stood for or simply looked upon him as a kindred cantankerous soul.

My father rose to speak to this point, and while he repeated to my mother, word for word, everything he had said and good summations of what his opponents had said, I see no purpose in setting it down here. Father hated guns and only accepted them as a burden we had to bear; closer to his heart was the war of ideas at a time of decision. I think that he deeply believed that if you could win an argument, you could win a war.

The final argument, as with almost all Committee meetings, revolved around the question of whether or not minutes should be kept.

As usual, after the timid ones—or sensible ones, depending on your point of view—had said their say to the effect that it was one thing to put your head in a noose and something else indeed to be your own hangman, my father rose to the occasion:

"I am a man of peace [so he told Mother, but it always appeared to me that he was the most belligerent man of peace I had ever encountered] yet on this point I rise in anger, indignation—and disappointment. Yes, disappointment! Are we slaves who plot and skulk in secret? Are we conspirators? Are we a pack of bandits, planning some dastardly thievery? Or are we free Englishmen, freeborn on our own freehold? Destroy the minutes? First I would cut out my heart and destroy it! Shall I be ashamed of this Committee? But if the Committee is not the noblest thing we have wrought, then how shall we face our brother Committees, scattered across these thirteen colonies? Destroy them? Give me the minutes, and I will bear them home with me, so that my children and their children may see that we did not fail to rise when history demanded it!"

As usual, Father's oratory carried the day, and the minutes remained where they always had been, on the top shelf of the Reverend's lectern, underneath his Bible. However, Mother asked Father, withal gently, whether he didn't think he had perhaps been a little strong in some of his denunciations and comparisons.

"Strong feelings demand strong words," he replied.

"Nevertheless, Moses, I would not want people to go around saying that you make mountains out of molehills."

"A mountain still in the distance can appear as a molehill."

"I suppose so. Still, I must confess that I like your reasonable moods better."

"And what was unreasonable about my opposition to burning the minutes? Are we animals, slaves, Frenchmen?"

"I didn't mean that at all, Moses. I simply meant that we will all be better and calmer and—don't be angry, please—happier when this blows over and our proper rights are granted to us."

Father could have found arguments; but he was tired enough to agree to this.

While Father was at the Committee meeting, I decided that I would walk over to the Simmons place. I needed sympathy, and Ruth was the most sympathetic person I knew. As a matter of fact, she was sympathetic to a fault, and sometimes it could be downright tiring; but in the mood I was in tonight, I couldn't have too much sympathy.

Cousin Simmons was a blacksmith. His father had been a blacksmith and his five sons were raised in the trade. Four of them pooled their capital and purchased half of the shares in a slaver that was running Africans from the West Coast into the Carolinas and the West Indies. There was divided opinion on the question of buying shares in slavers. These shares were handled by commission brokers in Boston and sold from a small shed on the river edge. Some held that since the slavers did not sail out of Boston Port, it was just business and no worse than any other business; and they bolstered their arguments by pointing to the abuses practiced on the sugar plantations and reminding their listeners that there was no Boston family of even modest means that did not have some stake in the rum trade. My father, on the other hand, held that slavers were the lowest form of life existent on earth, the devil in flesh, the Haman of our time. The Reverend agreed with him, and between them they carried the expulsion of Noah Cotton from the Committee after he invested five sovereigns in slaver shares.

That was no mean feat; and while most people accepted my father's position on moral grounds, the profits in slaver shares were enormous. Only one ship in three brought its cargo through, but when it did, the returns for the investor were magnificent.

The ship the Simmons brothers had invested in came through, making them rich as some folk consider riches, and they took the money and opened an ironworks in Connecticut. But Joseph Simmons broke with them and remained a smith in our village. He was a mild man, and you would never think to know him that he could be so adamant on a moral question—I, for one, have not found very much to admire in moral people, but he was an exception to the rule. His brothers were dead in his eyes; he would never speak about them or refer to them in any way. Lately, the British had ruined the iron business with their prohibitions, import laws and colonial taxes, and it had come to our knowledge that the four Simmons brothers had joined their local Committee and were real firebrands; but that made no difference to Joseph. As for Father, he never spoke openly about the various elements that went into Committees for various reasons, some of them less than noble, but I knew his opinion. He didn't hold them highly.

When I got to the Simmons place, the kitchen afterwork was done, and Mrs. Simmons and her widow sister Susan were sitting at the kitchen table reading Job aloud from the Bible. They were both of them sad ladies who dispensed smiles as if they were shillings, and they were strongly given to their Bible and to things like Job and Jeremiah and Nahum. It wasn't that they were unpleasant people; indeed, they were the sweetest things ever; they just enjoyed melancholy and seemed to take heart and spirit from it.

As I came in, Mrs. Simmons looked up and said, "Why, Adam Cooper, what a pleasant surprise!" Just as if she had not already seen me twice this day. The widow sister went to the cupboard and cut me a piece of sweet carrot pie; she was stronger for actions than for words.

"I just finished supper."

"Adam—that's my sweet carrot pie."

"Yes, ma'am," I nodded, and began to eat. It wasn't any effort at all.

"Adam has the finest reading voice," the widow sister said.

Mrs. Simmons nodded. "I remarked on that many times."

"We were reading from Job," the widow sister said.

"No matter how many times I read Job, I never fail to have a new insight. Do you find that to be the case with yourself, Adam?"

I had not paid much attention to Job lately, and mumbled something to that effect. As long as I kept my mouth full, they would accept anything I said.

"A shame."

"Such a shame," the widow sister said gently. "When we close our eyes, we are like the blind."

"I'm sure Adam would not willfully close his eyes."

"Not willfully, sister, but it happens."

"It would be nice," said Mrs. Simmons, "if after Adam finishes his pie, he would read to us aloud. It need not be Job. It could be Judges. I do think that there's more in Judges to interest a young man than in Job."

I appreciated her calling me a young man instead of a boy, and I also appreciated her substitution of Judges for Job. In its own way, Judges may be heavy going, but it does have a good battle scene or two, and it's just a sleigh ride compared to Job. But the last thing I wanted to do tonight was to spend it with a Bible reading, and I could have kissed Ruth when she came down just in time to get me out of the whole thing. Like the other Simmons women, Ruth is perhaps a trifle overgentle, but she has a mind of her own and she knows when to use it. She made no bones about letting them know that I had come over to see her and that we were going to take a walk in the moonlight.

It may seem strange that a churchgoing and pious woman like Mrs. Simmons should offer no objections to Ruth and myself walking after darkness, but Mrs. Simmons held that less was likely to happen at nighttime, when the grass was wet with dew and cold and clammy, than in the dry day under a hot sun. She was right.

All that happened between Ruth and me that evening was that we talked and held hands and kissed once. Ruth was three months younger than I, and I had known her since I had known anybody. When we were thirteen years old, she asked me whether I had decided whom I intended to marry, and I replied that I hadn't given the matter much thought since it did not appear to be particularly pressing. She was a little shocked at that, and I have since recognized that girls begin to brood upon these questions considerably before boys do. She, it appeared, had already thought the matter through and picked me—because she had always loved me and saw no reason why she should not continue to do so. After that, I had a few nervous days, but when I talked it over with Granny, she pointed out that empires could rise and fall before I came of marrying age and had to give the problem serious attention. I was vague on the process of empires, and not exactly sure what they consisted of, but nevertheless I was greatly relieved. It fell into the category of death from overeating, a fate I had been warned about on numerous occasions but which was far enough in the future not to trouble my sleep.

In the two years since then, Ruth changed considerably. She brought up the subject of matrimony less and less frequently, and finally dropped it entirely. At thirteen, she had been a skinny kid who, if not downright ugly, gave the general impression of two pale blue eyes behind a mass of freckles. She also ran to red elbows, skinned knees, and overlarge, bony hands. Since then, she had filled out very nicely; the elbows shaded down, and the bones were not noticeable. Her red hair, instead of flying wild like a mop upended, was gathered on her neck and highly admired by all sorts of people, and there were times when I found myself looking at her and thinking that she was beautiful. I will admit that my own attitude toward girls had changed, and there began to be occasions when I would say to Ruth:

"What I don't understand is why not, if you're going to marry me anyway?"

"You wouldn't understand because you're a boy and I'm a girl."

"My goodness, would I be pressing for that kind of thing if I was a girl? I should hope not!"

"And anyway, Adam Cooper, it's a long time since I said anything about marrying you."

"You haven't changed your mind?"

"Well, I don't know, the things you're always after! I just don't know."

But on this night, she seemed genuinely glad to see me. We got out of the house and walked down the lane toward the pump house. Then we turned toward the little grove of trees where Lyman's pigpen was, and we passed Mrs. Spencer, who said:

"Out walking, are you, Adam?" The way she said it made it totally sinful.

"Yes, ma'am."

"Well!" She could do a lot with one word. I had an opinion of her, but Ruth said she suffered from after-meal dyspepsia and had to walk around in the darkness to get the gas up, and it was a known fact that people with her condition were shorter and meaner than they had to be.

"Yes, ma'am, I'm sorry," I replied to Mrs. Spencer.

We walked on and Ruth remarked that she saw no reason for my apologizing to Mrs. Spencer.

"I suppose I'm just in the habit," I said. "I apologize to most anyone these days, and I'm pretty sick and tired of the whole thing, I can tell you that."

"There's no use to get morbid about it, Adam, I don't really care what you say to Goody Spencer or what she thinks. Have you been having a fight with your father again?"

"Still."

"What?"

"Not again—still. It's just one long affair. You'd think he'd want an hour here or there to rest himself from telling me what a useless, misbegotten thing I am. But not him. No, sir. It's like bread and butter to him. He thrives on it."

"Oh, Adam, it's not as bad as all that," Ruth said.

"Just tonight, I asked him as pleasant and respectful as possible whether I could go to the Committee meeting with him. Oh, no. When I was a man, I could go, and he made it plain to me what he thought about me being a man. Your pa was there, and believe me, I never was so humiliated in all my life."

"But you know about how Pa doesn't pay any attention to what Cousin Moses says."

"Gideon Perkins is three days younger than I am, and he's been attending Committee meetings since Christmastime."

"But wouldn't you rather be out walking with me, Adam?" Ruth asked, taking my arm. "If you were at the silly Committee meeting, you wouldn't be out here walking, would you?"

"I suppose not."

"Well, there."

"That doesn't make any sense, Ruth," I told her. "That doesn't solve one blessed thing."

"Adam Cooper, what do you expect to solve? You're only fifteen years old. Why don't you have enough patience to wait a few years and let things take their proper and natural course?"

"Maybe I will and maybe I won't."

"What does that mean?" she asked impatiently. Ruth Simmons had set ideas about what was fit conversation and action for a walking-out at nighttime, and this was not according to form.

"You know about my Uncle Ishmael Jamison?"

"The smuggler who keeps the colored wife in Jamaica?"

"Now that's a fine way to talk, Ruth Simmons! That's just a real fine way to talk! That shows a real profound knowledge of politics, yes it does! Just as if there was a master sails out of Boston without carrying a little contraband here and there! I suppose you'd want all our people to sit back and starve to death the way the British lords say we should—oh, yes, sir, yes, sir, we'll just wither away to please your excellencies, and go ahead and take all our churches and put in your priests and we'll all get down on our knees before those Episcopalian lords and padre them to death—"

"Well, I never!" she interrupted. "Indeed, I never—never in all my born days, Adam Cooper!"

"And as far as my Uncle Ishmael is concerned, there's not a word of truth in that story about him having a colored wife in Jamaica."

"Who cares!" she cried. "And who ever gave you the right to snap at me fit to bite my nose off?"

"I didn't snap at you. You—"

"He could have seven wives—he could be living with every loose woman in Kingston, for all that I care. Just make certain of that, Adam Cooper. I'm not like some folks I could name who will say the first thing they hear about someone else behind his back."

"Meaning me?"

"No, not meaning you. You don't have any more sense than a dry pumpkin."

"It was you called him a smuggler and a bigamist, wasn't it?"

"I did not. I simply identified him. For all I know, you could have five Uncle Ishmaels."

"It's not likely."

"Maybe it isn't. But it's a fine thing to have friends who can't trust you not to be a bigot!"

That was when I kissed her. We were standing alongside of the Hyams' well house, which sits behind their herb garden, and there was just enough starlight and night light for me to see her face, and it was hazy and lovely and only half real, and for that moment it appeared to me as the most beautiful woman's face I had ever seen in all my living days, not a girl's face, not the face of Ruth Simmons or anyone else I had known all my life, but the lovely face of a lovely stranger. When I kissed her, I felt that my heart would tear through my chest for excitement and wonder, and then I felt a good, empty sickness, if you can speak of anything in such contradictory terms.

"Why did you do that?" Ruth whispered.

"I don't know."

"Adam Cooper, if you aren't the strangest boy! First you're yelling and screaming at me as if I were heaven only knows what, and you're like to tear me to pieces. Then, without so much as by your leave, you kiss me."

I nodded, and she asked me why I was looking at her that way.

"What way?"

"The way you were looking at me."

"I just don't know." I wanted to tell her how beautiful she was, but how can you tell a girl something like that? And it didn't explain the way I was looking at her because I didn't know how I was looking at her.

"You seem to have forgotten all about your Uncle Ishmael," she said.

"Oh, no. No."

At that point, Mrs. Hyam opened her back door and called out, "Is that your voice I hear, Adam Cooper? I should think you'd have something better to do with your evenings than poking around well houses!"

So we walked again, and the moment that had come over me before faded, and Ruth was Ruth and looking pretty much as she had in her mother's kitchen. I told her how my Uncle Ishmael had offered me a place on his ship.

"Of course he would. He'd be glad to get you, instead of the trash he picks up on dockside."

"That's not a very flattering thing to say."

"Adam Cooper, I was just teasing you, if I must spell it out. You surely can't be serious about going to sea?"

"I don't know about that."

"Well, you can't. Your father never would let you."

"Maybe it's time I just went and did something without my father letting me or not letting me."

"Adam!"

"Why not? Would it make any difference to you?"

"Yes," she replied slowly. "Yes, it would. I suppose I'd be the loneliest girl in Massachusetts if you went away."

When she said that, I felt warm and good and content for the first time in days. I took her hand in mine. Her hand was small and soft, and the fingers twined themselves into mine. We walked down to the end of the lane and then back to her house.

When I got back to the house, I went into the kitchen, and there was my brother Levi sitting in

41

front of the hearth and cleaning my fowling piece with an oily rag. I let him know what for, and who gave him the right to touch my gun, much less clean it? Didn't he realize that he didn't have enough sense to clean a gun?

"I told him he could," Mother said.

"Well, suppose it was loaded? He could blow his head off."

"Wouldn't you like that," Levi grinned.

"It wasn't loaded," Mother said. "And if it wasn't dirty and gathering rust spots, Levi wouldn't be cleaning it. It sometimes seems to me, Adam, that you could take better care of your things. Your shoes will rot on your feet before you take some grease to them, and if I left it to you to change your shirt and pants, I don't think you'd take them off from season to season. I hate to scold you. I really do."

"It would be interesting to see what it would be like here if you enjoyed scolding me."

"Adam, I don't appreciate sarcasm."

"I'm sorry, Mother."

"The point is that Levi was trying to do something for you. He felt that you blamed him for what happened at the table, and he was trying to make it up to you."

"That's the blessed truth," Granny put in.

Levi sat on the edge of the hearth, looking downright virtuous. I shrugged and sat down next to him, and showed him how to clothe the ramrod properly for full cleaning.

"Adam," Levi asked me, "what would happen if you loaded this here gun with a musket ball instead of bird shot?"

"I don't know. I never thought of that. It's got a large bore that a regular musket ball wouldn't fill, and if you put an extra large ball in it, you'd have to put in an extra large powder load, and the skin of the gun maybe isn't strong enough to bear it. You might just blow yourself up."

"That's the trouble with a fowling piece. When I get me a gun, it's going to be a rifle."

"Ha! That's just like you, always talking when you don't know a thing."

"Of course not. You know everything, so there isn't anything left over for anyone else to know."

"At least, I know a little something about guns. Why, you couldn't even load a rifle—you got to hammer the charge home. And then, when you do that, what are you going to find around here that you could hit with a rifle? Chicken hawks? Squirrels? Partridge? Rabbit? Why, if you had any sense at all, you'd know that is precisely why a fowling piece was invented."

"I know one thing I could get with a rifle."

"You tell me."

"A redcoat soldier," Levi said slowly and seriously, and Mother turned to us from where she was sewing at the table with Granny, and said somberly:

"Levi, that's not the way anyone in this house talks!"

"All I said was—"

"I know exactly what you said. We don't talk about killing people in our house. We don't speculate upon it. We don't derive satisfaction from such inhuman speculation."

"My goodness, you'd think I was the only one!" Levi cried. "There isn't a boy in school don't keep score of how many redcoat soldiers he's going to get himself when the war comes!"

"That's enough," Mother said. "I haven't raised my children by the yardstick of boys in school, and I don't intend to begin now. We are not savages or barbarians, and we do not go to church to seek instruction in the art of killing. Now both of you put that gun away and march up to bed."

"I never opened my mouth," I protested.

"Both of you, Adam. It's close enough to bedtime in any case."

"I'm four years older than Levi. What sense does it make for both of us to go to bed at the same time?"

"I'm not disposed to argue," Mother said. That way, she was different from Father. He would have proved that it was right and proper for both of us to go to bed at the same time.

As we walked upstairs, I told Levi, "Among a dozen other things wrong with you, you never know when to keep your mouth shut."

I was a long time falling asleep that night, and lying there with the door open, I heard Father come in, and I heard his report to Mother concerning what went on at the Committee meeting. I have already set that down. When he finished talking about the Committee, she told him about the incident with the gun.

"I shouldn't have said what I said," Mother sighed. "At least, not that way. Adam is still a boy. Just because he's so tall and strong, we get to thinking about him as a man."

"It's time he thought about being a man," Father put in.

"We could both help him toward that."

"How? We've given him a good home, good food and good clothes, and an education. And if all goes well, he can go to college and board out with Aunt Martha in Cambridge. It doesn't seem to me that you can give a boy much more than that."

"Perhaps it isn't enough, Moses."

"How?" my father demanded indignantly.

"Well, he seems to have gotten the idea that you hate him."

"Hate him!" my father exploded. "Of all the crazy notions! Of all the idiotic ideas! There a boy, my first-born son—why, how could any man love a son any more than I love that boy? Now where could he have gotten an idea as unreasonable as that?"

"He could have gotten it from you," Granny said.

"Now see here, I won't have both of you turning against me. It doesn't mean a thing. You know the way boys are. I was somewhat sharp with him at the table, but boys get over that kind of thing. I'm old enough and wise enough now to thank the good God that my own father never spared the rod and spoiled the child."

"Age and wisdom don't go together as often as you might think," Granny said, "and as for your own father, Moses Cooper, I knew him better than you ever will. Abraham Cooper had many fine qualities, something I will not deny, but he was just as pigheaded and stubborn and enamored of the sound of his own voice as you are."

"Granny, you're being too hard on Moses," Mother put in.

"Oh, no—not at all, Goody Cooper. Like yourself, I was married to a Cooper, so I had double experience. Now you two can go on and make anything out of this that you wish. I shouldn't be interfering anyway, because it's provoking enough to have a mother-in-law in the home without her telling you how to raise up your children. I've said my say. Good night to both of you!"

They knew better than to interrupt or stop

Granny when she began to talk like that, and they sat quietly while she stamped upstairs. When she passed my door, I whispered:

"Granny?"

"And you, Adam Cooper," she hissed, "don't go thinking that because I scold my own son, I'm on your side."

"I love you anyway," I whispered.

"When I was young, a boy had modesty and decency, two qualities that seem to have disappeared today." She went on past into her room, and everything became so silent that I could hear the ticking of the big old clock on the staircase. Then from below, his voice considerably chastened, my father said:

"Well, Sarah, she is my mother."

"I don't see how it gives her the right to talk to you the way she does. You're a grown man, not a boy."

"She doesn't mean anything by it."

"Well, it's disrespect. I will not budge an inch from that. You're the man of the house. I said before and I say again—it is certainly disrespectful."

There were a few minutes of silence after that, and then Father said, "Come to think about it, I have been hard on the boy. That doesn't mean I don't love him. You know how much he means to me."

"Of course I do."

"I mean I got to disabuse him of that notion."

"Moses, if you keep building it up in your mind that way, you won't sleep a wink tonight."

"I just don't understand how he could form a notion that I don't care for him."

"You said yourself that those things don't last. Now give me a book and I'll read to you."

I heard Father get up and go into the sitting

room, and a moment or two later, in that high, clear, school-marm voice that she uses for reading aloud, Mother began chapter four of *Pilgrim's Progress*, which rated almost as highly in our house as the Bible, and most of which I knew by heart.

I fell asleep to the sound of her voice. My eyes were wet and my throat thick and full, but I think I felt better as I fell asleep than I had felt in a long time.

# The Night

I don't believe in dreams—that is, I don't believe that dreams amount to any more than tossing around the things that worry and provoke a body during his waking hours. Other folk are different and set a great store by dreams, picking them apart and developing them to distraction. I don't recall any event of importance, whether it was old man Higgens having a stroke, or the time a fox got in with the Phittses' chickens and killed eleven of them, that didn't produce a host of soothsayers, all claiming to have dreamed every detail in advance. I guess that if it proves anything, it only proves that what with everybody dreaming every night, there's always something for any occasion.

And thinking about it, I will admit that this point of view came from my father. Father liked to describe himself as a Christian-Judaic materialist. He held that if he just named himself a Christian, it was likely to take on at least some aspects of partnership with the Church of England. The Church of England was one of the things—one of the very few things, I should say—that he couldn't argue about. Not that he wasn't willing; but ten words after he began, his face flushed, his neck thickened, and he became near apoplectic. His mind ceased to function, and, as Granny put it, the worst elements of his father and grandfather emerged in him. There was a time when he could hardly get started on any subject without dragging in the Church of England, but since Mother had some High Church relatives on her father's side, he broke himself of that habit.

Granny said that to call himself Judaic when he had never actually met a Jew was impertinence, so when some family business took him to Rhode Island, he went out of his way to attend services at a synagogue. Father said that apart from the fact that they kept their hats on in church and read from the Bible in Hebrew—something he had always aspired to—they didn't seem any different from Presbyterians. While there, he couldn't resist getting their views on certain moot points of theology, such as the relationship of the Trinity to monotheism, and the balance of the first five books of the Bible against what follows. Not only did he emerge with a healthy respect for their powers of disputation, but he boasted of their admiration for his own powers of argumentation.

As for the materialism, Father held it was the only way to counter superstition properly, and high among the various superstitions that were an anathema to Father was the so-called interpretation of dreams. I remember an argument he had with Jonas Parker. Ever since Jonas Parker had been elected Captain of Militia for the township, things went less than smoothly between himself and my father—Father taking the point of view that the chairmanship of the Committee had precedence over all other titles of authority. Jonas Parker, with some justice on his side, said that a military situation demanded that the command of the militia be the supreme command at the moment of military crisis. You can imagine how my father rose to this; he hated all things military, and immediately accused Parker of desiring the prime goal of the enemy, to turn us into a garrison state. The argument was hot and heavy, with no clear-cut decision. Father awaited his moment. A day came when Parker announced militia drill for the following evening. My father reminded him that a strong, wet wind was blowing from the east, and that even in New England, where the weather was erratic enough to drive a prudent man mad, a steady, wet east wind meant rain. Well, up comes Parker with a particularly strong dream about the next day's weather being as fair as feathers, with a blue sky everywhere you looked.

"Now if that doesn't signify good weather, what does?" he demanded of Father.

"A dry west wind," Father replied. It rained that night and for the two following days, and Father had a time rending every theory of dreams into shreds. I agreed with him about dreams, so when my brother Levi ran into my room and dived into bed with me, trembling with fear over a nightmare, I was not disturbed, except that I resented being awakened in the middle of the night.

"Calm down," I said to him.

"The whole sky is red."

"It isn't." I pointed to the window. "If it was red, we'd see it from here, wouldn't we? Anyway, people aren't supposed to dream in colors. They say you dream in blacks and grays."

"I had a dream, Adam, that the whole sky was a terrible red, and I died."

"You can't dream you died. You'd never wake up if you did."

"Then I almost died. Are you mad at me?"

"Not any more. Go to bed."

"Why ain't you mad at me?"

"Look, Levi," I said. "I'm tired and sleepy. So why don't you go back to bed."

"Because I'm afraid."

"I'll tell you why you're afraid. I'll tell you why you dreamed that the sky was red. It's because you and all those other crazy kids spend all your time playing war. Bang, bang! There goes another redcoat. You have red on your mind even when you're asleep. That's why you dreamed that the sky is red." I got out of bed and pulled him over to the window. "Now look for yourself. Is the sky red or isn't it?"

Levi pressed close to me at the open window. We became silent as we stared out into the night. A few shreds of cloud lay across the moon, but plainly enough we could see the treetops, the common, Cousin Simmons' house, the Peabody house, and Buckman's Tavern, where the road to Menotomy bent around the common. It must have been about an hour past midnight then, perhaps a little earlier, but already the time of the night when silence settles like a heavy blanket, and a voice above a whisper is cursed and interdicted. I took comfort in the fact that Levi and I were sheltered by a strong house, with our mother and father nearby and with so many friends and neighbors within call. I have heard our relatives from Boston talk with some disdain about the few cultural offerings of a little town like ours, and about the bigotry and narrow-mindedness that is inevitable in a village, but at this moment I wouldn't have changed the security of my bedroom for all the wonders of the world. I can assure you that if you are thinking about going adventuring, or the sea and the wonders of far Cathay and the Indies, the middle of the night is no time for it.

Levi's skinny body was pressed up against mine, and I could feel him shivering under his night-shirt. I forced myself to be gruff and assured as I said to him, "There. Are you satisfied?"

"Adam—listen," he whispered.

He has ears like a bat. I listened, but I couldn't hear anything but the soft, sighing night noises.

"Adam, I hear hoofbeats."

"Well, suppose you do, Levi. There are travelers by night."

"Travelers don't race their horses in the darkness."

I heard it now, and Levi was right. The sound was of a horse being raced through the night, and clearer and clearer came the drumbeat of its hoofs. I strained my eyes toward the Menotomy Road, but it was too dark and there were too many trees obstructing my vision for me to make out a rider. But the rider was nearer now, and the hoofbeats echoed through the whole village; and then he pulled up in front of Buckman's, and I heard him shouting at the top of his lungs, although I couldn't make out his words. Being that Buckman's is a way station, they always keep night lights burning, and now lights began to flicker in the windows of the tavern. I heard the rider shouting again.

Father came into the room, pulling on his trousers over his nightshirt. "What are you boys doing at the window?" he asked.

Levi told him breathlessly.

"You're sure the rider was racing?"

We heard him shouting again. Mother came in, carrying a candle. Lights were beginning to flicker in some of the houses. "I don't see why," Mother said, "a rider by night must take us all out of our beds. You get under the covers this instant, Levi, or you'll take a death of cold from this night air." Granny then appeared behind her, demanding to know why everyone was up and about in the middle of the night.

"Is someone sick, Moses?"

"No one is sick," Father replied. "Why don't you all go back to bed?"

"Why don't you?" Mother countered.

"Now look, Sarah. That was an express from Cambridge. He came up the Menotomy Road, didn't he?"—turning to me.

"That's right."

"Well, if it's an express, it's Committee business. A man doesn't take a chance on breaking his neck on a dark, rutted road without it being a matter of some importance. And if it's Committee business, I have to be there."

Mother shook her head speechlessly, and Granny said that she might as well go downstairs and put up coffee, because it didn't look like there'd be much sleep in this house for the rest of the night. Father went back to his room to finish dressing, and Mother went downstairs after Granny.

I pulled on my shirt and trousers, and Levi wanted to know what I thought I was doing. Through the window, I could see lights in almost all of the houses by now. I told Levi that I had no intentions of missing whatever was going on out there.

"Then I'm getting dressed too," he said.

"It's no business of mine what you do. But Mother will pin your ears back."

"Not if you don't tell on me. I'll go out the window and down over the shed. You going to tell on me, Adam?"

"Oh, believe me, you're a fine one to talk about telling," I said to him. "Every time I take a step, you're there to play the rat. It would serve you right if I did tell."

"But you won't, will you, Adam?"

"I won't," I admitted, "but I won't lie either. If Mother asks me where you are, I'll tell her."

"Maybe she won't ask you," Levi said hopefully.

Father had just closed the door behind him when I got down to the kitchen, and Mother gave me one of her looks and said, "Well, I suppose it's morning, I suppose the good Lord forgot to bring the sun up this once but you know better. And just where do you think you're going, Adam Cooper?"

"Only over to the common, please, Mother."

"March right up to bed!"

"Mother," I said, slowly and carefully, "you know that I never disobeyed you."

"I should think not!"

"But if you don't let me go, I got to disobey you. Every house in the village is lit up and all the men are turning out for the common. You can't make me stay here."

"You're not—"

I think she was going to say that I was not a man, but Granny interrupted. It was the first time, as well as I could remember, that Granny had ever intruded into a discussion at odds between Mother and myself. She only said, quietly:

"I think Adam's right, Sarah. He ought to be there."

I imagine Mother was too shocked to reply. She nodded, and without allowing the matter to cool, I dashed out of the house and took off for the common. Middle of the night or not, the village was up and awake, and every man and boy in town was either already at the common or heading for it. When I reached there, a crowd had formed around the rider, packed around his horse about ten deep; and you could see from the way he sat on his saddle, proud as a king, that he was enjoying the attention. As far as we were concerned, he was the most important man in New England—important enough to make my father and Jonas Parker and the Reverend, the three of them at the horse's head, wait until he had finished draining a mug of beer that someone had passed up to him. When he finished the beer, he wiped his mouth with his sleeve and indicated his willingness to continue. He was a young fellow, and I noticed what a handsome pair of black riding boots he sported.

By then, I had wormed my way into the crowd. I had also gathered, from the talk around me, that he rode a warning express, that the British had marched out of Boston, and that a great army of them were headed this way, up from Charlestown to Cambridge and then on to Menotomy. I didn't believe it—not at first. For months and months, the talk had been that the British would send a force into our townships and put an end to the militia drilling and the Committee organization, but they never did, and somehow we had accepted the fact that they never would, and that all the hot talk would simmer down and that there would be a meeting of minds, what my father called "an intelligent and equitable settlement of all the points of dispute." Yet here was a rider telling us that a British army was coming.

"Now just one thing," my father was saying to him, "just one thing—what time did they start?"

"I told you they were getting into the boats to cross the Charles at ten o'clock."

"That's three hours ago. Did you wait until

they crossed the river? How long did it take them?"

"I waited until the first of them set onto dry land, I did— and they were forming up on the Menotomy Road. We just decided not to wait any longer."

"Well, what time was it then?" Parker demanded.

"Heavens to Holland, mister—what did you expect us to do? Build a fire so as we could read our clocks? All they had to do was catch sight of us, and that would be the end of any hope of my being here."

"Then you don't know what time they got across the river?"

"Well, just how long does it take an army to cross a river, mister?"

"That's what we're asking you," my father said with unusual patience.

"And I don't know—which is what I'm telling you."

"Did you come straight here?" the Reverend asked.

"By the Lord, I did, hell for leather—and I like to broke my neck on that pitch-black road. I'm here, ain't I? But I can't sit here all night. There was four of us, and one took off for Medford and another for Brookline and the third down to Watertown. You see, the meaning of it was that, one road or another, they'd be going to Concord where the stores are. Someone played the dirty rat and informed that the Committees were stashing away whatever they could put their hand on at Concord, so however they're coming, you can believe me that Concord is where they're headed at."

"But they wouldn't need an army for that," my father protested. "They wouldn't need an army just to confiscate the supplies at Concord."

"Don't argue with me, mister, please."

"Only how many troops?" Parker insisted. "Don't you see that we've got to know?"

"Mister, it was nighttime and we were hiding. Did you want me to count them?"

"A thousand—two thousand?"

"A thousand at least. Maybe two thousand, maybe more. They had a line of boats stretching across the river, and every boat packed full of redcoat soldiers. That's all I know—Now, make way for me. Let go of my reins, mister."

The crowd opened up for him, and he spurred his horse. He was a good rider, but wild and careless. He saw the common rail at the last minute and jumped it, sailed over it light as a feather, and then rode hallooing and shouting down the highway toward Concord.

After the rider had departed, the common showed signs of becoming the liveliest debating area in all New England. The central argument involved the Committeemen and the militia officers and the Reverend, who was torn between the Committee and the militia on one hand and God and the church on the other. The secondary arguments involved the male citizens who supported one faction or another. The final arguments were mostly between mothers and their children, involving the chill of the night air, the general lack of decent attire, and the effects of the loss of sleep. Along with these three major areas of dispute, there were many subareas where tempers ran high, individual duals between man and wife, mother and daughter, father and son—

all of it adding up to the briskest night scene I recollect in all my life. A dozen sputtering pine torches lit up the scene and gave it quality.

At the center of the dispute were four positions: Jonas Parker wanted an immediate muster of the militia. Since we had stored a hogshead of powder and another of lead shot in the cellar of Buckman's Tavern, Parker suggested that as our mustering point. Mr. Buckman agreed nervously. Everyone could see that his mind was oppressed with the question of whether each man would pay for food and drink consumed or whether it would be billed to the Committee. Things billed to the Committee had a way of being written off with a noble gesture, and there's nothing can be as destructive and disturbing to a small business man as a noble gesture.

My father, on the other hand, resisted a militia muster. It was incumbent upon him to take an antimilitarist position, and he bolstered his argument by suggesting the dangers of arming every sleepy citizen in the vicinity. Someone was bound to get hurt. Instead, he pressed for a Committee meeting in the church. If a redcoat army really was moving up the Menotomy Road, it couldn't move at much better than a snail's pace in the darkness, and we had plenty of time and there was no reason to lose our heads and jump to any wild conclusions.

The Reverend's position was that before we did anything, we should check the facts. I had half-suspected that he might put in a bid for a long prayer meeting, but all he desired was a practical approach to the problem. A number of citizens were pushing for an immediate ringing of the bells, just on the chance that someone in the neighborhood might still be enjoying his night's sleep, and the Reverend said:

"When the time comes for ringing the bells, we'll ring them, brothers, But let's just see where we stand before we go off half-cocked."

Sam Hodley stated the fourth position, that it was much ado about nothing, and not for a minute did he believe a wild tale about a British army marching up from Boston. It made no sense, he said. Anybody who knew the British knew that they didn't march at night. Why should they?

"To take us by surprise at Concord," someone said.

"What kind of surprise, when it's got to be dawn before they're halfway there?"

"The point I want to make," the Reverend said, "is this. Just for the sake of argument, suppose there is an army of a thousand men bound this way. Now that puts the question up to us, doesn't it? The muster roll of the Committee adds up to seventy-nine men—providing nobody's sick or absent. Now it's all very well to talk about our rights, but just what are we going to do with seventy-nine men facing a thousand? Good heavens, brothers, it's not like we had experience in this line of work. We are not soldiers. The only man in my congregation shot another is poor Israel Smith, when he put a load of bird shot into his brother Joash's sitting place, and I see Joash standing there, and he'll tell you it's not a rewarding experience, not for him who gives or for him who receives."

"I say amen to that," Joash Smith agreed.

If he had only put it a little differently, the Reverend would have had my father on his side. There was nothing my father loved better than an appeal to reason, and a nice point of logic just melted in his mouth. But somewhere in the Reverend's words, there was an implication of incompetence and even of cowardice. My father was just unreasonable enough to talk down the militia and defend the Committee in the same breath, and though militia and Committee were composed of exactly the same seventy-nine men, my father made a sharp distinction between them. The one, he held, was a quasi-military body, and nothing, he felt, adds to man's foolishness as much as playing soldier. The Committee, on the other hand, was a tribunal dedicated to unity, justice, and the rights of man—to use my father's own words—the finest form yet known in man's response to the call of his destiny. I admit this description is flowery, and a bit strong for anyone who had met our Committee face to face, but my father loved the Committee and cherished it.

But when the Reverend came straight out with his doubts concerning the odds, seventy-nine to a thousand, my father was caught on the twin horns of principle and militarism. Later that same night, Cousin Simmons remarked on my father's response; Cousin Simmons blamed the Reverend for a lack of faith, and noted that when the Reverend should have been invoking Gideon: "And the Lord said unto Gideon, The people that are with thee are too many for me to give the Midianites into their hands, lest Israel vaunt themselves against me, saying, Mine own hand hath saved me," he was instead meddling with the most temporal matters, namely the practical odds in a fight.

Father must have had the same thought in mind, and in any case, the principle waved like a flag. "Reverend," he said, "with all deference to your experience as a man of the cloth, you seem to have missed the point."

"How?" the Reverend demanded.

Everyone on the common perked up. Until now, the argument had been compounded out of confusion, uncertainty, and disbelief. But the ringing note in his voice—a tone Father reserved for the higher disputation—informed everyone that Moses Cooper stood firmly on a principle. Other men might have backed down, but next to my father, the Reverend was the most decisively opinionated man in the village, and the two of them at odds was worth walking a long way to see. The babble of voices died down, and the people pressed close around my father and the Reverend.

"Well, sir," Father said, "let me take up the way you put it, so that we understand the situation. Like yourself, for the sake of argumentation, I will assume that an undisclosed number of British troops have been ferried across the Charles River and are now making their way in the direction of this village. Granted?"

"Granted," snapped the Reverend. He never quibbled in an argument. He preferred to head in directly and lock horns.

"Whereupon," my father continued, "you qualify our rights and our duties by asking what seventy-nine men may be expected to do against a thousand?"

"I do. Indeed, I do."

"However, we don't know that a thousand men are marching here. It may be no men, fifty men, one hundred men, or two thousand men. As to numbers, we can only speculate. You will grant that, sir?"

"Granted. And come to the point, Brother Moses Cooper—come to the point, I say." He had a knit shawl over his shoulders, and he wrapped it closer about him. If the cloth had not called him, the Reverend would have made a great actor. He had only to raise one eyebrow and look down his long, pointed nose at you, to produce more effect than a hundred words.

"On the one hand a speculation—on the other hand a certainty."

"What certainty?" the Reverend demanded. He was becoming very impatient with Father—so impatient that he walked into the trap without ever seeing it.

"Our duty! Our oath in the holy name of freedom!" Father cracked out the words like a dead shot. "Is our principle flexible? Have we nurtured the Committee only to abandon it the moment it faces a test? Have we drilled a militia only to sweep it into hiding at the first glimpse of a thieving redcoat?" Father was taken; he could never resist the sound of his own words, and when he saw that the crowd was with him, he just couldn't bear to stop. "I say no! I say that right and justice are on our side! Who are these red-coated bandits that we should fear them? Are we strangers to the military curse that strangles England—the monster of conquest and blood lust that beckons us to equate the fat George with the antichrist? We know where they find their so-called soldiers, the sweepings of the filthy alleys of London, the population of their jails, the men condemned to the gallows and reprieved to teach us legality! We know them, and we fear them not! Our course remains the just cause!"

I felt like jumping up and cheering. It was as good as the best the Reverend had ever done on hell-fire and damnation, and it made my skin prickle and my hair stand on end just to listen. When the crowd let out a whoop, I whooped with the best of them. I was just as proud as punch.

Yet I think the Reverend's face was sad, and for some reason the fire went out of him. It wasn't like him to step down from a hot issue, but this time he did. He just nodded.

"I'm going to muster the militia, by God, I'm going to!" Jonas Parker cried.

"Can we have the bells, Reverend?" Cousin Simmons asked him.

He just nodded again, and half a dozen of the boys, myself among them, raced for the church, to have a hand in the ringing of the bells.

It's always fun to swing on the ropes and ring the bells, but to ring them in the middle of the night is so much of a treat that it's downright sinful. I felt that way. I guess that to some extent I had stopped thinking, and I was carried away by the rich sound of the bells pealing across the countryside. Before we rang the bells, there might have been some farmers on the outskirts of town who were still claiming their honest hours of sleep, but when we finished, I will swear that the whole blessed county was up and awake.

When we tired of the bells, Jonathan Crisp and Abel Loring, two boys who were a year or so older than I, came running up and told us that the militia were signing the muster book at Buckman's place, across the common. They had both signed and were on their way to their homes for weapons. When we heard that, the fever took us, and we promptly abandoned the

bells and made a rush toward Buckman's to get
our names onto the muster book. Halfway there,
Ephriam Holt's mother—he was no more than
thirteen—collared him and dragged him back to
their house. What she said to him doesn't bear
repeating, and while that was a matter between
herself and her son entirely, I don't approve of
some other things she said to us.

There was a crowd of men and boys, and a
good many girls and women too outside of Buckman's. The guest room of the tavern was lit up
and packed with just about as many as it could
hold, with the rest in front pressing to get in. I
saw Levi squirming his way into the crowd, and I
got hold of one arm and dragged him out.

"Just where do you think you're going?" I
asked him.

"I want to see the excitement, Adam."

"Don't you know that if Father catches sight
of you, you'll get more excitement than you can
bear? Does Mother know where you are?"

"No. I sneaked out over the shed."

"Oh, that's smart," I told him. "That's real
smart. She's just worried to distraction by now,
that's all—with you out in the middle of the
night and no idea where you are."

"Everyone else is out, Adam."

"All I can say is you'd better get home and
get home quick."

"What are you going to do, Adam?"

"Sign the muster book," I said, my mouth
dry.

Levi must have gone home then. At any rate
he was gone, and moving with the press of people I found myself in the entrance to the guest
room, or hostel room, as we sometimes called it,

of Buckman's. All around me were friends and neighbors, some of the men grinning when they caught my eye, but everyone warm and nervous and bound together by a thousand invisible threads, the way people become facing a great danger or excitement in common. It sometimes seems to me that we live inside of invisible shells, but just as much shells as the fat Maine lobsters inhabit; and only at a time like this do the shells melt away and the real people emerge.

Cousin Simmons saw me, pushed over, squeezed my elbow, and said softly, "A boy went to bed and a man awakened, hey, Adam?"

"I do hope so."

"Do me a favor, Adam?"

"Anything you say, Cousin Simmons."

"Your Cousin Ruth is out in all this commotion, and I don't blame the girl with everything stood topsy-turvy. Do find her and bring her home after you sign the muster book."

"I'll be pleased to, Cousin Simmons, but sure as the sunrise, I don't know whether I'll be signing that muster book. I just have my hopes and prayers."

"He's all bark and no bite. You should have learned that, Adam."

It's slow learning about your own father, I thought, and I said a prayer like this: Oh, don't let him do it to me in front of everyone standing here! Don't let him look at me the way he does, like I was nothing but a chicken thief caught in the act, and tell me that I'm no account and not fit to stand in with the men! I couldn't bear it now! I simply couldn't!

I was in the room now. There were at least six candles on the table where Father sat, with Jonas Parker on one side of him and Samuel

Hodley on the other. Jonas Parker had the muster book out in front of him, and when someone came to sign it, he would push it toward him and make a serious and almost ceremonial thing of the entry. Father had the minutes book of the Committee, and when someone signed the muster book, Father entered the name and the salient facts in the records of the Committee. It appeared pointless to me for two separate sets of records to be kept like that, yet I knew that most of the men agreed that the civil and military aspects of the matter should be cleanly separated. Samuel Hodley was the emergency storekeeper, and it was up to him to determine whether the militiaman had enough powder and shot; and if not, to see that it was issued. When a man had signed in, Jonas Parker would tell him:

"You are now on call and assignment until you are officially released from duty with a release signed by one of us three. In other words, you are now a member in good standing, under orders and in discipline in this Committee of Defense and Correspondence. Go home and get your gun and powder and shot, a pound of bread and a water bottle. Muster on the common at four o'clock in the morning."

I don't mean that he said that over and over, but enough times so that no one would fail to hear it. Even though I myself held to Samuel Hodley's opinion, that this was all a great bother and disturbance over nothing at all, his words made me feel cold and desolate for a moment.

I was in front of the table almost before I realized. "Name?" my father said briskly, in the official tone he used for Committee business—and then he looked up and saw me as I replied:

"Adam Cooper."

His eyes fixed on me, and I felt that they were boring inside of me and reading every thought. For myself, I had the feeling that I was looking at my father for the very first time, not seeing him as I had always seen him in the vague wholeness of age and distance, but looking at the face of a surprisingly young man, his wide, brown face serious and intent upon me, his dark eyes shadowed in their inquiry, his broad full-lipped mouth tight and thoughtful. How was it, I wondered, that I had never noticed before what a strikingly handsome man he was? How was it that I had seen in him only the strength of his overbearance and not the thewed strength of those massive brown arms spread on the desk with the white shirt sleeves rolled high and carelessly? It was no wonder that men listened to him and heeded his words.

The room was full of silence, and it stretched and stretched, and all the while my father never turned his eyes away from mine. What went through his mind I will never know, but I do know that time there became an eternity. At last, Father looked at Jonas Parker and nodded silently, and Parker pushed the muster book toward me. I bent over the table and signed my name, my hand trembling, the letters all blurred and wiggly.

"Powder and shot?" Hodley was asking me.

"Yes, sir."

Then I pushed my way out of the room, having no other desire than to be away from everyone else and for a while alone.

I walked around the common and back toward our house. By now, the town had begun to accept the fact that there would be no sleep for anyone tonight. Bells were tolling faintly from the directions of Lincoln and Menotomy, and all over the village there were voices, sharpened and increased, the way voices sound by night. There wasn't a house without lights in it, and in the kitchens you could see where the blaze had been built under porridge and coffee. It was a great holiday for the boys, and they were running back and forth, and shouting to each other and feeling just as important as fate. They shouted at me, but the fact of it was that I didn't feel like a boy any more.

I came up to our house by the back gate, which opens off the lane into the herb garden. About a year ago, Mother had gotten me to build a bench by the gate, maintaining that no gate was worth its salt or had any excuse for being if it didn't offer a resting place for a tired traveler. It wasn't much of a bench, because I was no great shakes as a carpenter, and I remember spending a whole day fitting the legs into the pegholes, but it was something to sit on and sturdy enough.

Ruth was sitting there now, and when I asked her what on earth she was doing, sitting there so calm and sedate in the middle of the night, she replied:

"Waiting for you, if you must know, Adam Cooper."

"Well, I made a promise to your father."

"Did you?"

"I said I would take you home."

"Really? Well, just in case you don't know, Adam Cooper, I know where my home is and I am capable of getting there."

"My goodness, all I did was say that I would

do something for Cousin Simmons because he was worried about you. That's no reason to chop my head off."

"Oh, sit down here by me," she said, "and don't make such a fuss."

"I can't sit down here with you, Ruth, and just spend time sitting like it was midday. I got a lot of things to do."

"Such as?"

"Well—things to do. You know, things." I sat down. I could see that she didn't intend to be easily satisfied, and I might as well be resting. Suddenly, I realized that I was tired and sleepy, and that there was nothing in the world I'd enjoy better than to crawl back under the covers.

"I saw you sign the muster book," Ruth said.

"Oh?"

"I'm frightened, Adam."

"Of what?"

"Don't you know? I know you have to pretend to be brave and manly, and not frightened one little bit."

"I'm not frightened, just sleepy."

"I get to feeling," she said, "that we're all asleep still, and this is just a dream."

"Well, I'll tell you what I think. I think it's all commotion and excitement and that's all. It doesn't make one bit of sense that the British are coming up with a real army. I mean, what for? I mean, why on earth would they want to start a war?"

"You always read about wars. But no one ever explains why a war starts. They just start. Suppose one starts tomorrow?"

"Well, suppose it did."

"You could be killed."

"I do not intend to be killed. Of all things,

Ruth Simmons—I think you're the one who ought to go back into bed and sleep. Let me just tell you—"

She didn't let me finish. She threw her arms around me and kissed me, and then held onto me as if she were drowning and I was a providential piece of wood. I was like to choke, but it did not seem proper to break away from her, and I waited until she let go and then suggested that I walk her home, since, as I had pointed out before, there were things I had to do.

"All right, Adam," she nodded.

We walked to her house in silence. I didn't go in with her. The way I felt, I couldn't face the prospect of her mother and aunt. Then I went to our house.

The kitchen door was open. Standing in the stormway I heard Mother say, "I don't care what your position was, Moses Cooper. I say you were wrong. There's some kind of madness in all this, and I know that I can't stop it or change it, but I can keep my son out of it. He's just a boy."

"Yesterday, he was a boy," Father replied, his voice dull and troubled. "Tonight, he's not."

"Now what kind of thing is that to say? That's exactly the kind of a thing a man says. I don't understand that kind of talk. A boy doesn't turn into a man overnight. It takes learning and growing and hurting. And most of all, it takes time."

"Sometimes," Father said slowly, "we don't have time."

"I'm sick and tired of this kind of talk. It's been going on too long, Moses, and you know it. What are we here? We're plain people. We live quietly, and we try to raise up our children properly and with a decent respect for God and man. We don't kill and we don't cheat. We don't have a jail in our town, and we haven't had a man in stocks since mid-winter. And now you tell me that we're going to fight a British army. I never heard such nonsense. You know that I never objected to Committee work, for all the time it took you away from your home and family. It was proper and just, and I had no call to go objecting to it. But when you tell me that plain, ordinary village people, men and boys that we've known all our lives, are going to try to stop an army—well, then I can only say that you and all the rest of them have taken leave of their senses entirely."

"You're making too much of it, Sarah," Father said. "I don't believe there's a British army coming—and even if they are coming, we're not going to fight them. Sarah, we're not going to commit suicide—and the British aren't our enemies that way. I know what kind of trash they fill their ranks with, but the officers are educated men. They're the same blood, and our language is common to us. Why, the last thing in the world that they want is bloodshed. We have a position and a principle, but it's not worth sixpence if we don't maintain it—and if they do come and see that we stand firm with some show of force, why, then they'll respect us. That's not the way to have bloodshed, but to avoid it."

"Then avoid it without Adam."

"How can I? Sarah, how can I? If you had been there when he came into Buckman's to sign for the muster—We had a line of folk. I didn't know he was there. But I looked up, and there he was. He didn't say anything. He just stood there and looked at me—and I tell you that his face said

more than all the words that ever passed between us. If I had forbade him to sign that muster book then and there, I would have lost a son.
Is that what you want? But I saw him there
so tall and strong I could have wept. You can't
shelter him now. You can't shield him. There
comes a time, and this is that time—"

I couldn't listen to any more. I went back
outside, and then I came back in, whistling and
making enough noise to let them know that I
was coming. They were silent when I entered the
kitchen. Granny was there, sitting in one corner,
looking smaller and older than ever. When I
came in, she shuffled to the hearth, and dipped
me a bowl of cornmeal mush out of a pot cooking
there.

Someone had to say something, and I asked
whether Levi had returned.

"He's up in bed," Father replied harshly.
"Where were you?"

"Let the boy eat," Granny said, putting the
bowl of mush on the table. "Do you want honey
on it or butter, Adam?"

Mother's face was like stone. She sat in her
chair with her hands clasped in her lap, and her
blue eyes were like agates.

"I'm not hungry, Granny. I can't eat."

She spooned honey onto the cornmeal, telling me that when a body was foolish enough to
stay awake all night, the best thing he could do
was to eat and bolster his strength somewhat.

"I just can't eat, Granny."

"I asked you where you were," Father said.

"Cousin Simmons asked me to find Ruth and
see her home."

"Did you?"

"Yes, sir."

"What are your intentions with Ruth, Adam?" he demanded—the last thing in the world I expected him to bring up tonight. "You're old enough to sign the muster book, to drive your mother to distraction, to stand up with the men with a gun in your hand—then you're old enough to stop being a boy with a girl and think of yourself as a man with a woman. Ruth Simmons is your second cousin once removed, so there's nothing to stop you looking at her with serious eyes, but be damned if I want you playing games with her by nighttime!"

I stared at him dumfounded and speechless, his tirade so unexpected, so uncalled for that I could not for the life of me either react to it or think of anything to say. It must have been the same case with Mother and Granny. The silence hung so heavy that I had to break it, move, do something, or burst into tears—the very last thing I wanted to do or could afford to do.

I went to the hearth where my gun was, and picked it up. I was trembling all over, yet bad as I felt I recall thinking what a good job Levi had made of the cleaning. The gun shone. There was no oil-film on it, but it had the proper oil touch that a well-wiped tool should have. I held it in my hands, my back toward the others, and I heard Father get up and walk over to me.

"Wrap a dry rag around the flint," he said hoarsely. "There's moisture in the night air."

"Yes sir," I whispered. "I thought to do so."

He was alongside of me, but I couldn't face him or look at him. "Is it loaded?"

"No, sir."

"Load it up. I want to watch you."

I nodded and took my powder bottle and measured out the cap measure for the muzzle.

"It's not enough," Father said harshly.

"It's the hunting measure."

"You're not hunting."

My mouth was dry. "How much?" I asked.

"Three times."

"It will kick like a mule."

"You can live with a bruised shoulder."

I added two more measures.

"How many pellets?" he demanded.

"Twenty."

"Do you count them?" he asked scornfully.

"Yes, sir—I count them."

"You'll stop to count pellets tomorrow? Is that it?"

"No, sir. I wasn't thinking."

"Then think!" he shouted. "Think! Use your head! Put your hand in the shot pouch and pull out a handful. Feel it in your hand."

I did so.

"Now count them."

There were twenty-seven pellets. I managed to say that it was a large load, that it could break the breech.

"Your breech isn't rusty and it won't break. Load them. Just remember what it feels like to count."

"Yes, sir," I said.

The gun was loaded. There were two loaves of bread on the table, each cut into three pieces. There were two water bottles. I stuffed the bread into my pockets, and slung a water bottle, a shot pouch, and a powder bottle over my neck. Father did the same. Mother and Granny sat there and never said a word.

"We muster on the common," Father said to them. "Close the shutters and stay inside until we return." Mother didn't move. Father shifted from foot to foot. Granny rose and went over to Father and pushed him to the door. "Go ahead now," she said. "It's no use standing here and making everybody fretful. Go out and wait there. I want to talk to Adam."

After Father walked out, I went over to Mother and kissed her on her cheek. She began to cry. I had never seen her cry before, and it had a bad effect on me. Granny took my hand and led me into the stormway.

"She'll be all right, Adam," Granny said. "Right now, there's nothing either of you can do for the other. Are you afraid?"

I nodded.

"I'm glad you can say that you are. Heaven help men like Moses Cooper who can't say it. I think that everything's going to be all right. God bless you. You're a troublesome and provoking boy, but I love you a good deal."

I squeezed her in my arms and kissed her, and finally I was crying too.

"Shame for those tears, Adam Cooper. Suppose the men see you?" She wiped my face with her apron, and then I went out to where Father was waiting in the herb garden.

# The Morning

It had become darker. There was a ragged veil of clouds over the moon and the stars, and my father bulked large and formless. I became tense with the feeling that perhaps it had already happened, that the British army was upon us, and that I would be left out of it; but whether I was pleased or dismayed, I hardly know.

We went through the gate, and without a word to each other, we began to walk over to the common. I noticed now that in many of the houses the lights were out, leaving only the ruddy glow of the kitchen fire. It was colder. I shivered and drew my jacket together.

A subtle change had come over the village. A little while ago, the night had been full of sound, the high-pitched sound of boys' voices against the flatter sound of their elders, the sound of bells, the sound of a rush and clatter and commotion and nervous laughter, but now all that kind of sound was gone. You heard single voices. Mrs. Carter called out to her husband:

"Jed! You forgot your notebook!"

Why on earth he wanted his notebook with him in the pitch blackness of night, I don't know. From somewhere else in the darkness, I heard the Reverend's deep voice telling someone to trust in the Almighty Maker. I sympathized with whoever it was. I have never been able to work up a feeling of being properly looked after, and it was worse in this darkness.

Father stopped at the edge of the common, and took hold of my arm. "Adam—" he began.

"Yes, sir?"

"I don't know how to say what I have got to say to you. I'm certain that nothing will happen. But something could happen, and you might have a heavy burden."

I nodded.

Then Father put his arm around my shoulder and held me to him for a moment. It was as close as he had ever come to a gesture of real affection and it made him uneasy and he began to complain about the night air and how it always gave him catarrh. We started across the common, and the Reverend joined us.

"Adam," he said to me, "I'm glad to see you with us. I have found that when adversity confronts them, the Cooper men stand firmly. God bless you."

It was a thoughtful thing to say, and it made me feel better. I suppose that when someone like the Reverend really applies himself to his job, he gets into the habit of saying the right thing at the right time—something I was never good at. It made me regretful that I had no predilection for the cloth.

"Would you know the time, Reverend?" my father asked.

"Close to four o'clock, I think."

The Reverend carried no gun or victuals, nor did he appear to be downcast. He put his arm through mine, and we walked toward the little cluster of men already gathered in the center of the common. At the same time, Cousin Simmons came from another direction, carrying an iron torch with a pitch cup at the top of it. He thrust this into the ground, and the flare of the pitch drove back the darkness and cast a circle of light upon the muster area. Already, at least

two-score men were present, and others were
coming by ones and twos from all directions. It
had seemed to me that what with the nighttime
and the distance some families were from the village, we would not muster more than fifty men,
but it turned out that before dawn seventy men
were on the common in the muster.

As we approached them, I noticed that they
were standing around in clusters, shivering a little in the predawn chill, trying to be casual and
make out that this kind of a nighttime call to
arms and muster was an ordinary thing that a
man might expect any night of the year. The
older men were talking about everything and anything, and the younger men and the boys were
listening; and those telling stories tried to
make themselves out as men of the world and
men of wide and varied experience, even though
everyone had known everyone else for the best
part of their lives and even though hardly anyone in the group had been much farther from
home than Boston or Providence. Caleb Harrington was telling the story—which I had heard in
one variation or another at least five times already—about the redcoat soldier who went into
the Rumpot in Boston and ordered boiled pudding and cheese. There was a great deal of disdain
among us concerning the wretched food the British seemed to enjoy and their lack of taste or
discrimination when it came to food. This tavernkeeper in the story was a sturdy Committeeman, and he brought the soldier a maize pudding
left over from the week before, and a cut of
cheddar cheese his wife had been saving for the
rattrap. Boston rats are known for their strong
stomachs. Well, the redcoat took a bite of the
pudding and swore some choice London oaths, and

said he had never tasted the like of it. The tavernkeeper told him it was Indian pudding, and begged him to try the cheese. The redcoat took a bite of the cheese and turned purple, and the tavernkeeper said it was Indian cheese and calculated to take the hair off your head. The redcoat was in a real fury by now and calling Colonials a colorful assortment of names. Now the tavernkeeper palmed an old scalp he had been keeping, leaned over the soldier, and came back holding up the scalp which he placed on the table. That was the kind of a story it was, and I thought it lacked humor as well as other things, but it raised a great laugh out of the men there. Someone else started another story immediately.

I saw Jonathan Crisp and Abel Loring, and I wondered whether I looked as small and cold and uneasy as they did. I went over to them, and we exchanged greetings very seriously. Abel Loring had a British supply musket, with the bayonet stuck in his belt. He was a year older than I, but much smaller, and he grinned sheepishly as he showed me the bayonet.

"I don't know what to do with it," he confessed.

"Can't you just see him sticking that into a redcoat belly?" Jonathan Crisp guffawed.

Abel Loring turned a shade white and admitted that the very thought of sticking it into anything made him want to throw up.

"He's done that already."

I never had liked Jonathan Crisp.

"The trouble is," said Abel, "that I'm afraid to sit down."

"Why don't you just throw it away?"

"I can't do that. It's Committee property."

Jonathan Crisp took out his pocket watch, a

present from his rich uncle on his mother's side, who was a chandler in Boston. "Ten minutes to four," he said, as if all the minutes in the hour were his own and exclusive possession.

Then the Cosden brothers came over to us, and I left them and walked over to where Father stood with Cousin Simmons, Jonas Parker, Samuel Hodley, Simon Casper and the Reverend. Simon Casper lived in Concord, but he had been on the long march to Quebec during the French War, and he had volunteered to help train the militia in our town. He had ridden over by night after the news reached him, and he had somehow found time to put on his old green army coat and his big cocked hat. He was the only one among us who had any semblance of a military appearance.

I stood a little distance away, still not completely certain that Father wouldn't change his mind. Either this was an unusually cold April night, or else any April night was provokingly cold when you went without sleep and spent your hours standing in a damp field. I pulled my jacket close and put my hands in my pockets, and when they closed around the bread, I suddenly felt starvation hungry and unable to endure another moment without eating.

We made good bread in our town. For one thing, the whole wheat berry was stone ground, not into fine flour but into a sort of meal. Mother kept a wooden sour tub, in which she mixed her dough and set it to rise. Every family had their own sour tub then, and that gave each bread its own character, each a little different from any other. Mother sweetened her bread with honey, salted it strongly for keeping, and mixed a wet dough. The finished loaf would be brown and heavy and damp inside, and would keep for ten days before it began to go dry and hard. I don't remember anything in all creation as good as that bread during the first few days after baking, and now I broke off small pieces and chewed them, holding my gun under my arm and hoping that no one would notice me.

As it turned out, there was no need for me to worry about Father recalling the unreliable elements of my character and deciding that I would do better home in bed than out here on the common, with a bird gun and my pockets full of bread. He had found a point of deep and constructive difference with Simon Casper. Simon Casper should have known that my father was bored to distraction with local argumentation.

For one thing, aside from the Reverend, there wasn't a man in town could stand up to Father and give and take properly in any dispute. Some of them, like Cousin Simmons, actually disliked arguments and attempted to avoid them whenever possible; others enjoyed a good dispute but were not equipped. And still others had been beaten to a mental pulp so often by Father that they avoided controversy with him the way a whipped dog avoids a fight. But Simon Casper hadn't been around enough for Father to take his measure properly, and when he suggested that the men stand ready with weapons at full cock, Father and the Reverend lined up shoulder to shoulder against him.

"There's nothing in the world more dangerous and uncertain than a cocked gun," Father stated.

"It's a case of preparedness," said Jonas Parker.

"For what?"

"For whatever's likely to happen," Casper said.

"Whatever's likely to happen, or even unlikely

to happen, is sure enough going to happen when you have a cocked gun in your hand."

"The point is," the Reverend put in, "that it mustn't happen." He raised his voice somewhat, so that anyone within a dozen paces could hear him. "The British are coming. That's right. We have more certain information than before. Two hours ago, they were forming up their ranks on this side of the river. We don't know exactly how many, but it could be almost a thousand men. Whatever my own thoughts on this matter were, it doesn't matter now. We have decided to spell out our principles with our presence. We have done no misdeeds, only stood by certain rights and privileges that are granted to us by the Almighty God and the struggles of our fathers. We are required to be firm and calm—but not to die. Ours is a way of life, not of death."

There were a good many "Amens," and I don't mind saying that the Reverend's words cheered me enormously, but Simon Casper wasn't satisfied. He said that if you were going to fight, you had to make up your mind about it.

"We're not here to start a war," Father said, "but to prevent one."

"Then we ought to take to cover and close the shutters behind us."

"All I'm asking," Father said, "is to avoid accidents. I'm saying that we don't cock guns or handle triggers. We show ourselves here, plain, firm, and quiet. We talk. This is our village and our land."

"You and I know that," Casper said. "But do the British?"

"And you aim to teach them that with a few dozen men against a thousand?" Father said with quiet contempt. "Let me tell you something,

Simon Casper." He waved an arm at the dark shadows of houses around the common. "Those are our homes, and inside them are our wives and children. So move gently before you come here with a war. Move gently."

He was disgusted with the man in the green coat. It was not even an argument. The Reverend drew him away, and I trailed after them. "Easier to let the devil out of the bottle," the Reverend said, "than to persuade him back inside."

"I hate fools. Blame the devil, Reverend, but I tell you that three-quarters of the misery of mankind is the result of plain damned foolishness." He drew out his watch and tried to see the hands. "What do you make it, Reverend? I have lost me a day somewhere. This is Wednesday morning?"

"Wednesday morning."

Father glanced at me briefly—as if to say something that he thought better of. In a low voice, the Reverend said to him:

"They were here tonight."

"Who?"

"Sam Adams and John Hancock."

"Oh, no," Father said. "Now what in heaven's name were they doing here?"

The Reverend shrugged, the gesture saying better than words that these were two men with their own ways.

"Where were they?"

"At my house."

"And now?"

"I didn't want them here," the Reverend said bitterly. "Would you want them here, Moses?"

"We got our troubles here."

"So it seemed to me. I can't understand any more how this started and the way it is building up. Who chose tonight? Ourselves? The devil? The British? No, I didn't want them here, and I told them to go to Burlington—"

"They left?"

"About an hour ago, Moses. They have their problems and we have ours."

Some of ours were approaching. Jonas Parker came over, with Samuel Hodley and Cousin Simmons trailing behind. Cousin Simmons came to me and put an arm around my shoulder. "It's a long night, Adam," he smiled.

"The longest."

"Are you angry, Moses?" Jonas Parker asked.

"I get impatient with stupidity, not angry," Father replied, but the other way around would have been fairer. He couldn't abide what he considered a stupid man, and he never stayed put long enough to qualify for impatience.

"No use calling this one stupid or that one smart. It's too late."

"That's a fact," the Reverend nodded.

"The point is," Jonas Parker went on, "that we ought to decide who is going to do the talking—the Committee or the militia."

"I thought you decided that," my father said. "I've noticed that a man with a gun usually shortens his arguments."

"That's no way to talk, Moses. You've got a gun and so has your son Adam."

"And I pray to God I'll not have to use it."

"As we all do," the Reverend said soothingly. "I think you'll grant, Moses, that Jonas here raised the question of a spokesman himself."

"That's fair enough," Cousin Simmons added.

My father appeared mollified, and offered a compromise. He and the Reverend would talk for everyone.

"I'd hardly call that a compromise," said Simon Casper, who had joined the group. "Why not one from the militia and one from the Committee?" Since he was a Concord man, it seemed to me that he was being a little pushy, and perhaps felt that he ought to be the spokesman for everyone. He was not a likable man. He made me nervous, and I think he made others nervous as well. But finally, they all settled on the Reverend. For one thing, he was unarmed, and would thus be in himself a physical proposal for a peaceful exchange. He would talk for the Committee, the town and the militia as well, since his congregation included practically everybody. I must say that I didn't envy him, having to stand out in front with no gun or way of defending himself, but he appeared to be relieved at the suggestion.

"There's only one thing that troubles me somewhat," the Reverend said. "Suppose they see us out here, but just decide to ignore us and march on past us up the road. After all, it's plain enough, from all I hear, that they're interested in Concord, where the stores are. Well, what then?"

"By God, then we stop them!" Simon Casper declared.

"Oh, man, use the brains God gave you," my father said, and Casper bristled and said he was sick and tired of listening to Moses Cooper's insults.

"When the day comes that plain discussion is characterized as insult, I'll move out of New England," Father snapped. "I'm only trying to make the point that there exists a certain disparity in the size of the forces concerned. The plain truth of the matter is that we can't stop them! What do you want, sir, a blood bath?"

Jonas Parker agreed. "Moses is right, Simon. My feeling is that we take up our positions here and hold them with dignity and courage. If they propose to march on past us, why, they march on past."

"Of all the damn things!"

Most of the militiamen were listening to the discussion now, and half a dozen side arguments broke out. Father shouted for silence. "Let's hear from the Reverend," he said. On the outskirts of the huddle, Jonathan Harrington, Caleb Harrington's seventeen-year-old son, began to play the *Redcoat Bangle* on his fife. "Jonathan, shut that pipe off!" his father shouted at him. The Reverend raised his arms, and when he got a little order, said to us:

"It seems to me that we haven't as many choices as some of us imagine. We are not here by choice, but because our consciences dictate that we assert our primacy in the place of our homes and birth. We are not soldiers and we are few in numbers, so I think we can end any discussion of fighting the British army, regardless of the ethic involved. However, we do have a role to perform, and we must see it through. In Boston, where we all of us have brother and sister, mother and father, aunt and uncle, and a hundred kin ties of blood and friendship, the British have seen fit to wipe out every vestige of freedom. They have taken quarters as they see fit. They imprison this one and that one as they please. They have shot down innocent men in cold blood. The streets are filled with drunken bullies in red coats —and there remains only a memory of what the city once was. It is not our choice but our necessity to prevent the same thing from happening here in the countryside, and we are drawn up here for that purpose. Here we stand with our arms in hand, but with no belligerence in our hearts. I do not think the British will pass by us. They have too much false pride for that. They will demand to know for what purpose we have gathered here, and someone must tell them. If you wish me to serve that purpose, I will try to compose my thoughts in whatever time is left to us—and then to state our purpose and integrity simply and directly. If you wish it so?"

I thought that it was beautifully put. I was cold and tired and hungry; still I admired that the Reverend, under such circumstances, could do near as well as he had done in church Sunday past. You must remember that he took off Friday and Saturday to prepare his Sunday sermon, and here was this, right off the top of his mind in the pitch-black night. I suppose that Father could have bettered it, being used to throwing in an argument at the drop of the hat, but for a reflective man like the Reverend, it was all one could ask. I even began to look forward to his projected exchange with the British, and to imagine some of the things I might say in his place. Just for the sake of peace, I hoped that his thoughts ran to less colorful language than mine.

When he finished, the applause came from all around, and it was plain that he had the sentiment with him. I can't express how relieved I felt. There is nothing that lessens one's warlike ardor more than a few hours in the wet and cold of the night, and with the reassurance of the Reverend that this would be no more than a polite and skillful exchange of words and principles, I began to anticipate the finish of it and work up a certain amount of indignation at whatever was holding up the arrival of the British. In all truth, I must admit that one of the things I felt I simply could not face was the possibility of being left out of whatever would happen. I could imagine the other boys talking about it and building up their own personal deeds, the way boys do, and strutting in front of the girls; and the thought that I might be out of all this was just heartbreaking. But now it would be all right. I would have my cake and eat it, so as to speak.

A number of the women and some of the younger boys had drifted out to the common. Jonas Parker and Simon Casper told them in no uncertain terms that they were to go home and stay out of the way. Then Jonas Parker yelled for the militia to fall into parade order and dress up. I had drilled with them enough to know what to do, and I found myself a place next to Abel Loring, in the second rank. Aside from Parker, Casper, Father, and the Reverend, sixty-six men had turned out for the muster. Even though there has been some argument as to the actual number, I know this for a fact—because once we were in rank, Parker had us count off, and the count came to exactly sixty-six. With the four men in front of rank, there were seventy of us assembled on the common, two lines of men, thirty-three in each line.

At first, there was something of a scramble on where they could get a good view of everything that happened, but even the Reverend agreed that the British would get a better impression of us if they saw mature men instead of boys, and he and Parker and Father and Casper went down the ranks, moving the boys back and the men up front. The one exception was Jonathan Harrington. He was seventeen but small for his age, and he didn't look much more than fourteen or fifteen, but he was a musician. The long-range plan was that we would have a regular corps of four drums and four fifes, and the Committee at Concord had been promising us the drums for weeks. But only one drum came through. Willie Diamond carried it until his mother drove him home and into bed. Abel Loring played the fife and so did Nathan Hamble. But Hamble was in bed with a bad sore throat, and Abel Loring had forgotten to bring his fife when he joined the muster. Jonathan Crisp and I pressed him to run home for it, but he was afraid that if he did, the British would turn up while he was gone and he'd miss all the fun. That left Jonathan Harrington as our only real musician, and he argued that there was no point in having a musician unless he played his piece where the enemy could see it.

His father was there, and I could see that he wasn't pleased with the notion of his son standing in front, when all the rest of us were in the back. Father didn't like the idea either. But Jonathan argued so hard and persistently that they gave way, and he took his place at one end of the front rank, just as proud as punch.

We stood facing east, and it must have been past five o'clock in the morning now, for when you looked at the eastern sky and then at the western sky, you could see how the one was lightening and the other still a deep charcoal lit brightly with stars.

The Reverend said to Jonathan Harrington, "Well, Jonathan, since your persistence has won your point, what can you play to ease our waiting?"

"Anything you say, sir."

"Would you render 'Old Hundred'?"

"Oh, yes, sir," Jonathan grinned. We all of us smiled a little when the Reverend mentioned "Old Hundred," just as we would have been disappointed if he hadn't. It was his favorite hymn. He still had in his house—I had seen it once— the original parchment sheet music that his folks had brought over from Old Amsterdam a hundred and fifty years ago, and which was supposed to have been hand-lettered by Henry Ainsworth; and there was almost never a Sunday when he didn't call for the singing of it. Now we took it up, all of us with full voice, so that they could hear it in the houses and know how high our spirits were, singing:

> "Show to Jehovah all the earth,
> Serve ye Jehovah with gladness;
> Before Him come with singing mirth;
> Know the Jehovah He, God, is!"

It was strange, but after we sang the one hymn, a pall fell upon us. I know that I was thinking about Jonathan Harrington, and how he had been talking of marriage with Bessie Suderland, and I thought how terrible it would be if he should be struck down, standing as he was in the first row, and how would Bessie Suderland feel? It was a foolish way to think. I looked at the men and boys around me, and their faces were gray and drawn and old in the predawn. The whole eastern sky was grey now; we were a part of it; and the gray lay in dew upon the grass of the common. My belly was queasy, but out of fatigue not out of fear; and I told myself that the British would not come. Had we made fools of ourselves? How did the men feel, standing here in the lines on the common, with every manner of weapon, bird guns, muskets, matchlocks, rifles, and even an old blunderbuss that Ephraim Drake insisted was the best weapon ever invented.

Then Father and Jonas Parker walked down our line and reminded everyone to see that their flints were not on cock. They didn't want any accidents, they said. Father looked at me, and smiled and nodded, and that picked up my spirits a good deal. I took the bit of flannel off my flint.

Far in the distance, shots were fired. We heard them. The sound was like twigs snapping in the winter frost. Everyone became tense, and men leaning on their guns picked them up and held them in both hands.

In the west, the dark band of night washed away. The birds began to sing around the common, the way they do in the hour before dawn. A cloud high in the sky turned pink with the first reflection of sun, but the east, the direction of the Menotomy Road, was still full of haze and mist.

And then, after all the waiting, all the climax and the anticlimax of the long night, the British came and dawn came. Men who were talking dropped their voices to whispers, and then the whispers stopped, and in the distance, through the morning mist, we heard the beat of the British drums. It began as a rustle. Then it was the sound of a boy running through the reeds of a dry swamp. Then it was my own sound as I ran along a picket fence with a stick, and how did I come to be here, grown, with a gun in my wet hands? Fear began. I felt it prickle on my spine. I felt it like a weight in my belly. I felt it like a sickness around my heart, and its accompaniment was the steady, increasing roll of the redcoat drums.

The Reverend smiled and pointed to Jonathan Harrington, who whistled up the tune of "Come Swallow Your Bumpers," a song that everyone was singing in Boston and through the country; but no one sang, not even the Reverend. Jonathan Harrington played on alone, but then he stopped playing as the redcoats came marching out of the lifting mist. Then we were silent and tight, tight as strings drawn to the snapping point, and my hands hurt as they gripped the gun. Many of the men half raised their guns and bent a little, but we boys looked at each other and licked our lips and tried to smile. And in front of our lines, Jonas Parker, my father, Simon Casper, and the Reverend moved closer together.

When the British saw us, they were on the road past Buckman's. First, there were three officers on horseback. Then two flag-bearers, one carrying the regimental flag and the other bearing the British colors. Then a corps of eight drums. Then rank after rank of the redcoats, stretching back on the road and into the curtain of mist, and emerging from the mist constantly, so that they appeared to be an endless force and an endless number. It was dreamlike and not very believable, and it caused me to turn and look at the houses around the common, to see whether all the rest of what we were, our mothers and sisters and brothers and grandparents, were watching the same thing we watched. My impression was that the houses had appeared by magic, for I could only remember looking around in the darkness and seeing nothing where now all the houses stood—and the houses were dead and silent, every shutter closed and bolted, every door and storm door closed and barred. Never before had I seen the houses like that, not in the worst cold or the worst storms.

And the redcoats did not quicken their pace or slow it, but marched up the road with the same even pace, up to the edge of the common; and when they were there, one of the officers held up his arm—and the drums stopped and the soldiers stopped, the line of soldiers stretching all the way down the road and into the dissipating mist. They were about one hundred and fifty paces away from us.

The three officers sat on their horses, studying us. The morning air was cold and clean and sharp, and I could see their faces and the faces of the redcoat soldiers behind them, the black bands of their knapsacks, the glitter of their buckles. Their coats were red as fire, but their light trousers were stained and dirty from the march.

Then, one of the officers sang out to them, "Fix bayonets!" and all down the line, the bayonets sparkled in the morning sun, and we heard the ring of metal against metal as they were clamped onto the guns.

One of the officers spurred his horse, and holding it at hard check, cantered onto the common with great style, rode past us and back in a circle to the others. He was smiling, but his smile was a sneer; and I looked then at my father, whose face was hard as rock—hard and gray with the stubble of morning beard upon it. I touched my own smooth cheeks, and when I glanced at the men near me, found myself amazed by the shadow of beard on their faces. I don't know why I was amazed, but I was.

Then another British officer—I discovered afterward that he was Major Pitcairn—called out orders: "Columns right!" and then, "By the left flank," and, "Drums to the rear!" The drummers stood still and beat their drums, and the redcoats marched past them smartly, wheeling and parading across the common, while the three mounted officers spurred over the grass at a sharp canter, straight across our front and then back, reining in their prancing horses to face us. Meanwhile, the redcoats marched onto the common, the first company wheeling to face us when it was past our front of thirty-three men, the second company repeating the exercise, until they made a wall of red coats across the common, with no more than thirty or forty paces separating us. Even so close, they were unreal; only their guns were real, and their glittering bayonets too—and suddenly, I realized, and I believed that everyone else around me realized, that this was not to be an exercise or a parade or an argument, but something undreamed of and unimagined.

I think the Reverend was beginning to speak when Major Pitcairn drove down on him so that he had to leap aside. My father clutched the Reverend's arm to keep him from falling, and wheeling his horse, Major Pitcairn checked the beast so that it pawed at the air and neighed shrilly. The Reverend was speaking again, but no one heard his words or remembered them. The redcoats were grinning; small, pinched faces under the white wigs—they grinned at us. Leaning over his horse, Major Pitcairn screamed at us:

"Lay down your arms, you lousy bastards! Disperse, do you hear me! Disperse, you lousy peasant scum! Clear the way, do you hear me! Get off the King's green!"

At least, those were the words that I seem to remember. Others remembered differently; but the way he screamed, in his strange London accent, with all the motion and excitement, with his horse rearing and kicking at the Reverend and Father, with the drums beating again and the fixed bayonets glittering in the sunshine, it's a wonder that any of his words remained with us.

Yet for all that, this was a point where everything appeared to happen slowly. Abel Loring clutched my arm and said dryly, "Adam, Adam, Adam." He let go of his gun and it fell to the ground. "Pick it up," I said to him, watching Father, who pulled the Reverend into the protection of his body. Jonas Parker turned to us and cried at us:

"Steady! Steady! Now just hold steady!"

We still stood in our two lines, our guns butt end on the ground or held loosely in our hands.

Major Pitcairn spurred his horse and raced between the lines. Somewhere, away from us, a shot sounded. A redcoat soldier raised his musket, leveled it at Father, and fired. My father clutched at his breast, then crumpled to the ground like an empty sack and lay with his face in the grass. I screamed. I was two. One part of me was screaming; another part of me looked at Father and grasped my gun in aching hands. Then the whole British front burst into a roar of sound and flame and smoke, and our whole world crashed at us, and broke into little pieces that fell around our ears, and came to an end; and

the roaring, screaming noise was like the jubila-
tion of the damned.

I ran. I was filled with fear, saturated with
it, sick with it. Everyone else was running. The
boys were running and the men were running.
Our two lines were gone, and now it was only
men and boys running in every direction that
was away from the British, across the common
and away from the British.

I tripped and fell into the drainage ditch,
banged my head hard enough to shake me back
to some reality, pulled myself up, and saw Samuel
Hodley standing above me with a ragged hole in
his neck, the blood pouring down over his white
shirt. We looked at each other, then he fell dead
into the ditch. I vomited convulsively, and then,
kneeling there, looked back across the common.
The British were advancing at a run through a
ragged curtain of smoke. There was nothing to
oppose them or stop them. Except for the crumpled figures of the dead, lying here and there,
our militia was gone. The last of them were
running toward the edge of the common, except
for one man, Jonas Parker, who staggered along
holding his belly, his hands soaking red with the
blood that dripped through them. Two redcoat
soldiers raced for him, and the one who reached
him first drove his bayonet with all his plung-
ing force into Parker's back.

"Oh, no!" I screamed. "Oh, God—no! No! No!"

Then I saw redcoats coming at a trot on the
other side of the ditch and, through my sickness and terror and horror, realized somehow that
if I remained here, I would be trapped—and it
was not death I was afraid of or being taken by
them or getting a musket ball, but that thin,

glittering bayonet going into my vitals or tearing through my back the way it had with Jonas Parker. So I leaped up and ran, still holding onto my gun without ever knowing that I held it. The soldiers saw me and ran to cut me off, but I fled past them, across the common, leaped the fence, and ran between two shuttered, blind houses and tumbled down behind a pile of split kindling, and crouched there, vomiting again, over and over, until my chest and shoulders ached with the convulsive effort of it. Then I ran behind the house and another house, and there was the Harrington smokehouse, and I hid in there, with the hams and butts and sides of bacon over me. I crawled into a corner, put my face in my hands, and lay there sobbing.

At fifteen, you can still manufacture a fantasy and believe it for at least a few moments; and I had need for such a fantasy, or I would lose my wits and senses completely; so I began to tell myself that none of this had happened, that it was all something I had invented and dreamed, that I had never at all awakened during the night, that my father was not dead and that the others were not dead. I didn't believe any of this fantasy, you must understand; I knew that I was inventing it; but I had to invent it and use it to get hold of myself and to stop the screaming and pounding inside of my head. In that way, it worked. I was able to stop my convulsive sobbing, and to sit with my back to the smokehouse wall and just cry normally. Once I had established a fantasy about my father being alive, I was able to break it down and argue with myself, and then accept the fact that Father was dead.

He was dead. He had been shot by a musket ball, and if that had not killed him, then a bayonet had been driven into him the way I saw the bayonet driven into Jonas Parker. No one had fallen down on the common and lived. I knew that. We had made a mistake. We were stupid people. We were narrow people. We were provincial people. But over and above everything, we were civilized people, which was the core of everything. We were going to argue with the British, and talk them out of whatever they intended. We knew we could do that. We were the most reasonable, talkative people in all probabilities that the world had ever seen, and we knew we could win an argument with the British hands down. Why, no one on our side had even thought of firing a gun, because when you came right down to it, we didn't like guns and did not believe in them. Yes, we drilled on the common and had all sorts of fine notions about defending our rights and our liberties, but that didn't change our attitude about guns and killing. That British Major Pitcairn on his champing horse knew exactly what we were and how we thought. He knew it better than we knew it ourselves.

And now my father was dead. It was so absolute it closed over me like a blanket of lead. He would never come home again. He had put his arm about me the night before, and had given me such a feeling of love and closeness as I had never known in all my life; but he wouldn't do it again. He was like Samuel Hodley, with the blood pouring out of him; and I began to think of how much blood a man has, and you just never know that a man can bleed so much, a red river coming out of him, until you see it happen—and then I began to think about Mother, and ask myself whether she and Granny and Levi had watched the whole thing from the upstairs windows, and how they had felt when they saw it happen. If you could dig the deepest well in the world and call it misery. You could find the place of my feelings then. I sat there and cried. I hadn't cried so much since I was a small boy, very small, because a boy gets over crying early in a town like ours.

"God have mercy on me," I said to myself. "I am losing my mind, and soon I'll be no better than Halfwit Jephthah in Concord, who is sixty years old with the brains of a five-year-old, and now I, myself, am hearing voices." I was hearing voices. I heard a thin, cracked voice wailing, "Adam! Adam Cooper—are you around? Are you alive?"

I opened the door of the smokehouse, and there across the yard was my brother Levi.

"Levi," I whispered.

He jumped like a startled rabbit and looked all around him.

"Levi! Here in the smokehouse!"

Then he saw me in the open door, ran to me, and threw himself sobbing into my arms, hanging onto me as if I was the only thing left in the whole world. He was crying now fit to break his heart, and that dried up the tears in me. I have noticed that when you have two brothers in a difficult situation and one begins to cry, the other usually contains himself. That was the way it happened to me. I pulled him into the smokehouse, closed the door behind us, and said:

"What are you doing out here?"

"Looking for you."

"Well who sent you to look for me?"

"Granny did. Adam, Father's dead."

"How do you know?"

"I saw him dead," he sobbed. "He had two bullet holes in his chest. They shot him dead, Adam. Those lousy rotten redcoats shot him dead. That's my father. They shot him dead, Adam." He was shivering and shaking. I shook him until he had calmed down and was crying evenly again. Then I put my arm around him and squeezed him, the way Father had done to me, to show him that I wasn't angry.

"Where did you see Father?" I asked him.

"Out on the common. Granny and Mother ran out there and I went with them. First the redcoats tried to stop us, but Granny was so wild and terrible angry that they let her go, and she fell down on her knees where Father was lying and began begging him he shouldn't be dead, because out of five sons, he was the last one. But Mother just grabbed onto me and held me and looked at Father, and just wailing and wailing quiet, like a little girl—oh, it was terrible, terrible, Adam. It was just more terrible than anything, just more terrible, Adam, I tell you. Then a redcoat soldier came over, and he said something to Mother about could he help—I don't know exactly what he said, because you can't understand them so good the way they speak, and Granny stood up and spit in his face and said things to him like I never heard her say before. Goody Simmons was there and her sister, and the four of them, they picked up Father and carried him in to the house. And there were dead people all over the common, with the women crying and wailing, and the redcoat soldiers all over everywhere—"

"Who else was dead?" I whispered.

"I don't know all of them—I didn't look. Some of them were across the common, and there were two men lying in the drainage ditch, I think one of those was Jonas Parker. Caleb Harrington is dead. Then I saw Jonathan Harrington crawling along through his own blood, the blood was running out under him, and there were some women trying to help him, and he was crying. Isaac Muzzy was lying next to Father. He was dead. He was all cut with bayonets and they had smashed in his head."

He began to shake again, and I held him for a while and quieted him.

"They killed Father," he said. "Father's dead, Adam. Did you know that?"

"I know that, Levi," I said softly. "But he didn't feel any hurt or pain out of it. I saw how they shot him. It never hurt him at all."

"It hurts to be dead."

"No, it doesn't."

"How do you know?"

"I know, I know," I said. "Stop shaking. Everything is going to be all right."

"It'll never be all right again. Father's dead."

"Well, people die. People die. Don't you think Father knew that he could die when he went out there to stand up to the British?"

"Then why did he go?"

"He had to go," I told him. "He had to go."

"Why didn't you kill the British?"

He had asked it finally, and then someone else and then someone else—and they would never stop asking why no one, not one of us, fired his gun, not one shot, not one show of force or courage or anything like that—but only the running away.

He must have felt it in me in the darkness, and he said:

"I didn't mean that, Adam."

"It wouldn't make Father alive," I muttered. "Father's dead. We have to think of what to do."

"He had two holes in his chest," Levi said.

"What did Granny say to you?"

"They laid him down on the dining-room table. Goody Simmons began to wash him. His face was dirty and bloody. But Mother just stood there and said, 'Moses Cooper, Moses Cooper—'"

"Don't keep on talking about it and thinking about it."

"He's dead."

"What did Granny tell you to say to me? Can I come home?"

"You can't come home. There are redcoats all over the place. She says to hide in the woods back of Cousin Simmons' house until darkness falls. Then we can hide you in the house."

Yes, I thought, I'll hide in the house and hide in the woodshed, and even if I come out into the sunshine one day, I'll still be hiding.

"Will you do that, Adam?"

"Tell them not to worry about me. I'll be all right."

"You wouldn't run away, Adam?" he begged me. "You wouldn't run away and leave me all alone?"

"Of course not."

We sat quietly in the darkness for a few minutes. Levi pressed close to me, pushing his face into my jacket. He felt small and helpless, and I was filled with guilt for all the times we had quarreled and all the names we had called each other; and I told myself that from now on, I would take care of him just as if I were his own father.

"You'd better go home now," I said to him. "I guess it's bad enough at home with all the misery they got, without worrying about what happened to you and me."

"What shall I tell them?"

"I'll come later, when it's safe. I'll be all right. I'll take care of myself."

But when Levi slipped out of the smokehouse, I was alone again and afraid again, and no one to come between myself and my fear and grief.

# The Forenoon

I must have dozed off for just a moment or two, and I was awakened by the sound of voices. I crept to the door of the smokehouse and put my eye against a thin crack in the closing, and there, no more than three or four paces away, were two redcoats, standing there in the morning sunshine and looking, or so it appeared to me, directly at me.

"Now take that shed, Sergeant," said one of them. "It could be stuffed as full with Yankees as a goose with pudding, and us none the wiser."

"You have a point there, Blythe, indeed."

"Or that woodpile there."

"A possibility, no doubt."

"They are tricky devils, they are."

"Not to be trusted."

"I would sooner trust my wife."

"There you have the nature of them, Blythe. Sly. Sly as women. You and me could be standing there, having a word with each other, just two honest men attempting to do their duty according to a solemn oath they have sworn to the King, and they'd like as not be planning to pot us from that window up there."

"The devil!"

"I don't say it's so. I say it could be so."

"Then just inform me, Sergeant, why we don't take a torch to the whole dirty pile and burn it to the ground?"

"That's not for you and me to decide, Blythe. That is in the nature of policy."

A third redcoat joined them, and said, "The

Captain says to stand to parade on the common, Sergeant. We are marching."

"Marching?"

"That's what the Captain said. Marching."

"And without a wink of sleep."

"I say it's a shame, and I don't care who hears that. There is enough feather bolsters in this town to bed down the regiment."

"I am merely communicating orders, Sergeant."

The three of them walked out of my area of view, and then I heard the sound of bugles and the rattle of drums. Whether all the redcoats were marching, or whether it was only their regiment, with another regiment left to guard and search the town, I had no idea. But when I opened the door a few inches, it was clear as far as I could see, and I felt that this was my chance to get out of the trap of the smokehouse.

You might think that with my father dead, my own fear would have lessened; but it didn't work that way, and all I knew was that I was alone—and who would take care of me or see for me now unless it was myself? When they spoke of burning the place, I saw myself trapped in the shed, roasting to death. I only wanted to get out of there and go where I might never see a redcoat again.

So, with the coast clear, I leaped out. Still hanging onto my gun, I raced across the back yard and garden of the house, down a little slope, and plunged into a fringe of woods there, never glancing behind me or even to the side, but only eager to find the cover of the brush. It was still too early in the season for bushes and underbrush to be in leaf and provide cover, and the skin of woods was only about thirty paces across. But just beyond it, there was a stone wall, and behind the stone wall, I would have shelter, with the open meadows as a place of retreat.

But no sooner had I plunged through the woods than I almost ran into two redcoats, who were making their way along the stone wall. When they saw me, one of them let out a cry for me to halt, and the other threw up his musket and fired. I wasn't more than twenty feet from him, so he might well have hit me if his piece had fired; but it flashed in the pan without taking in the chamber, and I sailed over that wall as if I had wings. Once in the open meadow, I had no fear that they could catch me. I had long legs, and many was the foot race I had won, but the redcoats were burdened by their heavy uniforms, their enormous muskets, and the big packs they wore on their backs. I stretched my legs and fled across that meadow as if the devil himself were after me—and I felt that way too—holding my speed for the quarter of a mile that separated me from the stone wall that bound the opposite side of the meadow. There, panting, exhausted, I fell across the wall into two arms that embraced me like a steel vise.

I clawed and twisted and struggled and tried in every way I knew to break that hold until I was brought back to sanity by a voice in my ear telling me:

"Easy, easy, easy, my lad. I have no desire to harm you. I only don't want you exploding that bird gun in my face out of your excitement. Excitement is a bad state for a body. Many a good man would be alive today, if he weren't dead from excitement. Now just take a good look at me. My name is Solomon Chandler, out of Lincoln Town, and I come across the meadows to see you running like a deer in flight. But them two red-coats you fled from, they are standing back there, and none too quick to come across the meadows a-hunting us. Just look and see, and be calm."

I relaxed, and he let go of me, and sure enough, back on the other side of the field, the redcoats were standing and watching, but making no move to come after me.

"And if they should take a notion to come," said Solomon Chandler, "do we want to turn our backs to them?—or maybe to keep a cool head on our shoulders, since we are two to two, even odds, my lad, and a gun is a commoner, an equalizer, believe me."

I stared at him now. He was a tall man, a full head taller than I was, and long in his arms and his legs and skinny as a starved crow. But it didn't weaken him, being skinny; I had felt his grip and knew that. He had a long face, a long hooked nose, a jutting chin, and two pale blue eyes, deep-sunk in their sockets. When he smiled, he showed a mouthful of broken yellow teeth, with wide gaps between them. He wore a provision bag over one shoulder, a powder horn, a bag of shot and a water bottle over the other, and he carried a rifle as tall as he was. His hair was snow-white, and altogether he was the most freckled man I had ever seen and possibly the ugliest.

"You don't know them!" I gasped, still trying to get back my breath. "You don't know them! You don't know what they did over there! We were standing on the common and they fired on us! They shot us down like dogs! They killed my father!"

"Ah, no—Jehovah damn them! Did they do that? Did they kill your father, your own blood?"

I nodded, and all my control went, and I burst into tears and put my face in my hands and cried like a little boy, full of shame and sick all through, but unable to halt my crying.

"Now that's the right thing," said Solomon Chandler. "Let the tears run freely. Grief should not be denied. Cry until you are free of it, boy. The Almighty knows that you have reason for it. Don't be ashamed for me. I have six children and nineteen grandchildren, and each one of them is as dear to me as you were to your own father, may he rest in peace."

I was able to stop then, and I was grateful to him, for as strange as his words were, they calmed me and soothed me—as if for the first time I actually realized that life would continue, and that my father's death and what had happened in our village did not mean the end of everything. Glancing across the wall, I saw that the two British soldiers were gone. Solomon Chandler was asking my name.

"Adam Cooper."

"Adam Cooper. All right, Adam, my boy, suppose we walk a spell and put a mile between them redcoats and us, and then we'll just sit for a bit, and you will tell me what happened back there." He reached into his waistcoat pocket and took out a silver watch. "Twelve minutes after nine," he said, "and you've lost your youth and come to manhood, all in a few hours, Adam Cooper. Oh, that's painful. That is indeed."

"I wish it was true that I have come to manhood," I said bitterly.

"Give it time, Adam. Give it time."

And then he set off with a long, brisk stride. I had to half-run to keep up with him. He set off westward, and for about a mile, we walked parallel to the Concord Road. Then we turned south into the woods, climbed a hillock, and came to a tiny, grassy glade, screened from every side by brush and wood. I had thought that I knew all the countryside hereabouts, but Solomon Chandler knew it better than I did, every field and fence and coppice. Once we were in the glade, he asked me whether I was hungry, and when I nodded, opened his provision bag and took out of it cold roast chicken, a piece of ham, bread, and a boiled fruit pudding. He spread a cloth on the ground, laid out the food, cutting it up so that I should have no hesitancy about helping myself, and then pressed me to eat.

I felt that it was wrong of me to be so hungry. I felt that it was sinful, in the face of all that I had seen and all that had happened; but after I had tasted the first bite of food, I ate as ravenously as a starving man. I suppose it was my hunger and the circumstances that made it so, yet the food tasted better than anything I had ever eaten. Between the two of us, we finished the ham and the chicken and the fruit pudding, washing it down with water from our bottles. Only some of the bread remained, and this Solomon Chandler wrapped carefully and stowed back in his provision bag. Then he stretched his legs and his arms and said to me:

"Now, Adam, confess that you feel a trifle better?"

I nodded.

"Life is potent, Adam. If it wasn't, you and I wouldn't be sitting here. You witnessed a mighty terrible thing, but men are clever when it comes to doing sinful and beastly things to other men, and what you witnessed was not the first time and it won't be the last either. But life has a special quality of asserting itself, and that's a very important thing to learn about, it is."

"My father's dead. Talking like this won't bring him back."

"That it won't, Adam—be sure of that. Nothing's going to bring him back. You know, laddie, when a young man like yourself first watches the death of someone close and dear to him, it's a bitter shock, it is. But if it was you lying out there on the common and your father out here, then there would be no consolation whatsoever, none at all that I could offer. The natural way is to let the old go, let the young live and taste life. Your father went too soon, but oh, my heavens, laddie, life is only a day, a long, long day, but that's all. I am sixty-one years old, and it's like yesterday that I was a boy your own age, and a year older when I shipped out of Boston Town to see the whole world, and then back to be married and raise my own, and then off to the French War—and all of it comes down to a moment. The Lord God Jehovah, He is eternal and timeless, He that was and is and always will be— but you and me, laddie, we have a little bit to do and we do it as best we know how, and that's just about as much as you can say for us or for your good father, may his soul rest. Now I have said enough. I could sit here and talk you deaf, dumb, and blind, I could. But I want you to talk to me. I want you to tell me what went on back there and just how it happened—all of it, how it began and then everything that transpired."

He was not to be resisted, this old man, Solomon Chandler. He never raised his voice, and everything he said had a trace of apology in it; yet

I found myself telling him every detail of the previous night, how the rider came to warn us, how we assembled on the common and how the British came. I left out none of it, nor did I attempt to polish it up and make us out to be heroes of any kind. I told him that so far as I could see, not one shot was fired from our side. I told him what kind of cowards we were, and how we ran as if the devil himself was behind each one of us.

When I had finished, he remained silent for a while, and I could see that he was thinking over all that I had said. Meanwhile, he had taken an old black pipe out of his pocket and a plug of tobacco just as black. Thoughtfully, he shaved tobacco off the plug and stuffed the pipe. I was wondering whether he'd kindle a fire to light the pipe, but after he had taken a draw or two on it, he put it back in his pocket unlit and unsmoked.

"Cowards, you were, Adam?" he asked at last.

"Yes—cowards."

"Oh? I think you got something to learn, laddie, about the nature of cowardice and bravery. It takes no courage to fire a gun and to kill, merely a state of mind that makes killing possible. Such a state of mind does not come easily to decent folk. But we will see." He rose to his feet and picked up his long rifle. "Come along now, Adam—if you're minded to throw in your lot with me."

"I can't go home now."

"Then come along, boy."

"Where?"

"In good time—all in good time. You know where the Mill Brook forks?"

"I know the place, yes."

"Well, son, there's a little pasture south of it where I imagine we'll find a few sturdy Middlesex lads. It's a long way ahead of us, and what's started ain't easily finished."

We set off again, Solomon Chandler walking more slowly now, and we cut across the fields, over stone walls, and through bits of woods—but still more or less paralleling the Concord Road. North of us, we heard the sound of drums and the shrilling of pipes, faint at first but then clearer; and the sudden panic in me was eased by Chandler's hand on my shoulder.

"Easy, easy, boy," he said. "Their music never hurt a living soul, and you just make up your mind to stroll along just as casual as if you was out walking with your lassie. If you have one now. Do you?"

I nodded.

"Tell me her name."

"Ruth Simmons," I whispered.

"Then that would be Joseph Simmons' daughter, him the smith back there. Am I right?"

"Yes, sir."

"Bless my heart. Now, do you know, Adam, the last time I set eyes on her, she came no higher than my kneecap. And what kind of lovers are you? Are you betrothed?"

"I'm too young to be betrothed."

"Oh, bite your tongue with such words! How old are you, boy?"

"Fifteen," I answered.

"Fifteen. Now in my own days, that was never too young for a betrothal, or for a marriage either; but we're a careful lot these days, and they say a lad should have this and that before he takes him a lady. Myself, I was married at seventeen years, and never regretted it—good heavens, no. And you're a big, upstanding lad. To look at you, I would have said you were seventeen at least."

"Johnny Harrington was seventeen, and they killed him on the common."

"Take your mind off such things now, Adam," he said gently. "Don't worry the dead. Let them lie in peace." We had topped a little hill, and there, half a mile to the north of us and plainly visible, was the highroad. His arm over my shoulder, Solomon Chandler paused there and pointed toward the long column of redcoats, stretching up and down the whole length of the road that was in our view. At this distance, they were like toy soldiers, small, harmless, and impersonal.

"Have a good, long look at them, Adam. It's a healthy business to regard what you fear. Look at it long and calm, and you will find that it calms you inside."

I did as he said, and bit by bit, the panic in me worked out; my heart beat less strongly, and the awful, mindless fear of them began to subside. While this was taking place inside of me, Solomon Chandler talked on, his tone as chatty and comfortable as if we were sitting in Mother's kitchen and not out here in the open with the redcoats only half a mile away.

"Study them, Adam," he said, "and realize their stupidity and ignorance. They have a great contempt for us, and they call us peasants and louts, but not one in ten of them can read or write his letters. A good half of them are convicts, cutthroats and footpads, serving out their time in His Majesty's colors instead of in jail. The rest of them are poor, ignorant devils, with a religion as cloudy and superstitious as their minds. They are a poor substitute for machines.

They do what they are told to do, and when there is no one to tell them, the life goes out of them."

"Where are they marching?"

"To Concord, no doubt, having heard that we put some shot and gunpowder away there. But it will be easier going there than coming back. Each of them carries his Brown Bess, fifteen pounds of regulation musket that I would not give you sixpence for. Mind you, they don't even have a back sight on that gun of theirs. It's a handy tool for a bayonet and murderous when they stand up against you as they did on the common, but a single shot will never find you. They don't know how to aim the thing. It kicks like a mule, but the bullet carries only a hundred paces. And the pack on their backs weighs forty pounds more. Five pounds of shot and water, a heavy spun uniform, canvas leggings, and a wig under that fool hat they wear. Oh, yes, indeed —it will be easier going than coming."

"We won't try to stop them then?"

"Oh, no, Adam—not at all. It was a shame that a terrible thing had to happen at your home, but we won't try to stop them now. Let them march. There are good boys at Concord to move away whatever must be saved, and there will be good boys at the old North Bridge too, if they should desire to cross it. All in good time, and we'll be going along now."

We marched off again, the old man walking as easily and casually as if there were no redcoat within twenty miles, instead of a thousand of them a stone's throw away; and I must say that it had its effect upon me. I could feel my mood changing. Where my whole body and every thought had been saturated with grief for my father, now I could feel that same grief hardening like a knot in my belly. Whatever lay ahead of me, I at least began to sense that I would be able to face it; and the old man seemed to know the change in me. He nodded approvingly and said:

"We are an old race of people, Adam, and there is not any fear that can't be faced and dealt with. Make yourself compatible with it, and it shrivels. That's been our way this long time. You might ask yourself, How does old Solomon Chandler know what he knows about the British? Well, I went a-soldiering with them all through the French War, and I learned some knowledge of them, believe me. You know what they called me, laddie?"

"They call us damn Yankees."

"That's the new learning. Then they called us gillies, which is a Scot word for peasant. Hey, you suffering, thick-headed gillie, damn you! That was a common form of polite address by their officers, who looked down upon us with contempt, in that we were not gentlemen. The artful ways they had! There was one of them, a captain or something of the sort, who once asked my opinion on a matter of the weather. I answered him, It will be fair weather, Jehovah willing—and then he says back to me, What the devil are you gillies, Jews or something, with your damn Jew names and your talk of Jehovah this and Jehovah that?"

"And what did you say to that?" I wanted to know.

"Tell you, Adam—I am slow to retort. A man's better for thinking a bit before he says his piece, and I looked at that redcoat man, up and down, I looked at him, and then I said very quiet and gentle to him, It is only by the mercy of that same Lord God Jehovah that I don't cut your throat. He saw that I meant it, too."

"And did he bother you for it, Solomon?"

"Heavens, no. He became a gentleman, like he was born and bred to be."

We came to the lane that runs north and south, from Lincoln Town to the Concord Road, and I remembered how, only the autumn before, Father and I had been out hunting in the hours after dawn, and I shot two fat rabbits south on the lane, and we were nigh freezing to death when we got to Cousin Joshua Dover's house in Lincoln, and there it was for the first time that I had a good drink of hot rum, beat up with butter and sugar.

The day before this, I could remember nothing about Father but the birchings and his anger and sarcasm; it was curious that now I recalled so many good things, and discovered that the bad things were not so bad after all.

Today, as we reached the lane, which was sometimes called the Lincoln Lane and sometimes the Indian Trace, we saw nine men walking up it from the south, all of them with guns and sober faces; and we waited there in the lane for them. Some of them I knew by sight, and one of them was Cousin Joshua Dover and another was his nineteen-year-old son, Mattathias. They grinned when they recognized me, and then they saw from my face that something bitter and sad had happened. We would have our Thanksgiving dinners usually together with the Dovers and the Simmonses and with the family of Mother's brother, Simon Hatch, so I knew the Dovers well enough. Mattathias took me out with my bird

gun the very first day I used it, and instructed
me on how to load it and prime it. He was a
heavy, slow-moving person, but kind and soft in
speech, just as his father was. His father had
studied for the pulpit but given it up later to
take over his grandfather's store and flour mill,
yet he kept on studying and had the reputation
of being the finest Hebrew Scholar in Middlesex
County. I had heard Father say that he maintained a correspondence with ministers all over
New England, and that he was the most con-
sulted man in the colonies, when it came to subtle and confusing interpretations of text, and
had even made a number of journeys to Providence to check his facts against the old scrolls
that the Jews kept there.

When he saw the expression on my face, he
went straight to me and took me by the arms,
Solomon Chandler meanwhile explaining the circumstances of our meeting and something about
what had happened.

"Your father?" Cousin Dover asked.

"They shot him down dead." I didn't cry again,
I was finished with that. I felt cold and bleak,
but I also felt that whatever I did from here
on would be done because I willed it so, not because I was a boy who couldn't control his
emotions.

"I think you had best tell them all about it,
hard as it is, Adam," Solomon Chandler said.

So I told the story again, but more shortly
now, and harder and crisper with the things that
had happened. I was angry now. It was a slow
thing, this beginning of anger inside of me, and
it was not until afterwards that I knew it was
happening and growing and curdling.

When I finished, there was a silence as heavy

as sorrow, and no movement or motion but the pressure of Cousin Dover's arm around my shoulder—just the silence in the pretty country lane, with the bees humming about their spring work and the birds singing and the west wind sighing —and faint, ever so faint in the distance, the rattle of British drums.

They absorbed it and digested it, and then they composed themselves to it and mixed their horror and anger and indignation. And then they asked questions with the quiet uncertainty of people visiting the home of a friend who had died.

"How many of our people were slain?"

"I don't know."

"Can you guess, boy?"

"Maybe eight, ten, twenty—there's no way for me to tell."

"Do you know some for certain?"

"Some."

"What were their names, boy?"

"Caleb Harrington, his son Jonathan, Jonas Parker—he was militia leader for our town—Samuel Hodley, and my father. Maybe the Reverend was slain, I'm not sure."

Their faces became even harder, and one or two of them rubbed their eyes and stared at the ground.

"You're sure there was no provocation from us?"

"I saw none. Our guns weren't cocked. Father and the Reverend, they insisted that the guns be not cocked, and that would prevent accidents from happening."

"So they started it."

"No matter now," another said.

"It's the finishing now."

"Is the news off to Waverly?" Solomon Chandler asked.

"We sent a rider off with the first gunfire."

"Where's the assembly, Solomon?" asked Cousin Dover.

"Where we planned for it. South of the Mill Brook fork in Ashley's Pasture. So come along, I say, come along."

Eleven of us now, we marched on, following the cow track that led from the lane to Atkins' farm. At the farm, there were Levi Atkins, his brother, Seth, his father, old Moses Atkins, and the four Atkins boys. They were armed and ready, and apparently they had been waiting a long while for the men from Lincoln Town.

Now there were eighteen of us, and we cut through the Hancock Woods toward the Mill Brook. When we came out of the woods, I could have cried out with joy, for there were Cousins Simmons and the Reverend and Tom Dover.

I don't know how I can explain what that meant to me. It doesn't make much sense for me to say that after what had happened on the common, I had the feeling that the whole village had died—not only the dead men who lay on the common, but the whole village dead and gone and never again to be the way it was. It was a heavy and sad feeling, combining with the loss of my father, the loss of everyone else who was dear to me. And when I saw Cousin Simmons and the others from home, that broke and went away; and without shame or care for who was watching, I threw myself into his big arms and let him hold me as tight as if I was a little shaver and he my own father. Then I thought he'd break my ribs, the way he clutched me in those blacksmith arms of his, and when he let go of me, I saw that the tears were pouring down his cheeks.

"God be praised!" he said.

The people who were with me watched respectfully. We were not used to war and death in those days. We were plain people, and nothing like this had ever happened to us before. Solomon Chandler took off his hat, shook hands with the Reverend, and suggested that this would be an appropriate time for some sort of benediction. The Reverend wiped his eyes and nodded. Those wearing hats removed them, and the Reverend said quietly:

"For thy everlasting mercy, Almighty God, we thank thee."

Then the hats went back on, and we struck out for Ashley's Pasture. I heard one of the men from Lincoln comment that it was a short and peculiar benediction, and that he didn't think much of a preacher who couldn't draw some moral out of the events of today. But I guess the Reverend could be excused. He had been through a lot, and I know that he had always been fond of me, even though I once overheard him telling Mother that when it came to plain, downright intelligence, I couldn't hold a candle to my younger brother Levi.

We were twenty-one strong when we reached Ashley's Pasture, and there were over thirty men there already and waiting for us, and while we remained there, during the next hour, men kept coming in to join us, by ones and twos and threes—so that eventually there were at least a hundred of us gathered there. They had several breakfast fires going, and the first thing Solomon Chandler and other smokers did was to get hot coals to start their pipes. While the Reverend

never actually came out and condemned smoking
as part of the devil's witchery, he did take a
very dim view of the practice, and no one in our
home had ever smoked. However, when Solomon
Chandler offered me a draw on his pipe, I didn't
refuse. I guess it was that morning that I became a smoker.

# The Midday

The Reverend never let a Sunday go by without imploring his congregation to fear God, and that was one of the matters I used to brood upon as a part of passing the time in church. I don't think that anyone with a fairly honest recollection of his childhood will fail to admit that time passes more slowly at meeting than anywhere else, unless perhaps—as I've heard some say—in jail. And one of the things that always plagued me in church was that, no matter how hard I worked at it, I couldn't truthfully say that I feared God. The way I saw it, He simply did not rate with Father or Mother or darkness or the witch's house behind the meetinghouse, or the schoolmaster, or old, cantankerous Gideon Phaile, who hated children so much he always whacked away at them with his stick when they came within reach—not with any of them as an object to be feared.

If we had been High Church, like some of our more distant relatives in Boston, and had prayed to an impersonal and elegant God, I might have come to the proper attitude; but the Reverend clung to Jehovah as the proper name for what he softly and lovingly would describe as "the Ancient of Days," and somehow or other, the name Jehovah invoked no menace at all. If one of Mother's seafaring relatives had turned up and been introduced to me as Jehovah Hatch, I would have considered it natural and not impious. Also, I once overheard Father and the Reverend discussing this very matter, and Father leaned to the opinion that our race—meaning Presbyterians, and some Congregationalists and some Quakers, but mostly Presbyterians—were not afraid of God but of women. "We have established the new matriarchy," he said, and that led me to Granny for an explanation of what the word meant. "It means your father never grew up," she said, but then went on to explain it properly. I subsequently decided that there was a good deal of truth in what Father said.

In any case, I have never seen men really relaxed unless they were in a position secure from intrusion by women. No matter how hard and bad their case might be, they took it as a holiday; and even though what had happened in our town cast a pall over everyone at Ashley's Pasture, the evil tidings of the massacre could not wholly dissipate the feeling among the people. Something had happened, and more would happen, but here it was in between in the April sunshine and as balmy and sweet a day as Massachusetts had ever known. I felt aggrieved at first that they were not weeping with me in my sorrow, but then I remembered what Solomon Chandler had said and tried to comfort myself with the fact that life continued. I was beginning to understand, though vaguely, that it must continue, even if our common was to become the common of every town in Middlesex.

The men were all in little groups of relatives and neighbors, some of them toasting bacon over the fires, some cleaning their weapons, some just sprawled out comfortably and chatting. Many of them stopped to say a kind word to me as I passed among them, and here and there, and increasingly so, were men from home who had stood with me through the night on the common. I was amazed at how many were alive and turning up here, for somehow I had the impression that most of us had been slain in the first fire. Plainly, this was not the case.

From what I heard, listening to this group and that one, there were six assembly points spotted between the Menotomy Road and the Watertown Road. That was to give the Committeemen gathered at these various points the freedom to move north or south, depending upon what road they had to cover. Meanwhile, the Committeemen from west of the Sudbury River and west of the Concord River would converge on the North Bridge, to hold the western bank of the river there. The British would reach Concord, if they had not reached it already, but they would go no further—and after what had happened at the common, some of the men maintained that it would be just as well if the British remained there.

More and more, I began to understand what an amazing piece of organization my father and the other Committeemen had carried out. It was true that no one was shouting orders, that men just drifted in from every direction, without appearing to be in much of a hurry about it, and that the hundred-odd men sprawled about in the pasture looked as unlike an army as anything you might conceive of; but nevertheless they were carrying out their purpose with a calm that astonished me, and they were where they had to be with time enough to spare.

There were a number of men who wore the blue and white ribbon of the militia officer on their hats, and they kept coming to Solomon Chandler, who sat on a bit of stone wall with my

Cousin Dover from Lincoln Town. Cousin Dover was trying to make a tally in a small black notebook he carried in his pocket, checking off names with a quill pen. His ink was balanced on a rock, and he sat on the stone wall as serious and businesslike as if he were in the store back at Lincoln and going over his accounts. Meanwhile, Israel Thatcher, the news carrier from Medford, was selling his papers and gathering news to piece together the story of the massacre, and questioning everyone who had been on the common. He attempted to borrow Cousin Dover's pen and ink and notebook, arguing that an accurate history of the day was more important than any muster book; but Cousin Dover informed him that he would do better to wait until the day was over before he wrote its history, and unless someone had enough sense to bother with a muster book, it might make poor history indeed. Further, he implied that he didn't think very much of a news carrier who would come out on a day like this one without some writing materials.

Cousin Simmons had a cold meat pie in his jacket pocket, and he insisted that I share it with him. I tried to explain that Solomon Chandler had shared a whole provision bag with me, but that wouldn't satisfy him a bit. He just knew that I'd feel better if I ate something, so I took half of the pie just to please him. As a matter of fact, after the first bite I enjoyed it thoroughly. I had never considered Goody Simmons to be much of a cook, but I must say that she did an old-fashioned meat pie as well as anyone.

"I guess Moses is dead," he said to me. "There's no doubt, is there?"

"No, sir. They brought him into the house."

"Who did?"

"Mother and Granny and Cousin Rebecca."

I told him about the smokehouse and how Levi had found me there; and then he took hold of my hands and told me, plain and quiet, that while nothing could ever replace Moses Cooper in my heart, I could turn to him just as I would to a father. It meant a good deal to me to hear him say that, because he was not just saying it. He meant it. It wasn't very easy to get to know Joseph Simmons. He was one of those big, heavy-muscled, slow-speaking men who seem to think through every word they utter; but once he set his mind to something, he did it, no matter what price he had to pay, and if he gave his word, he kept his word. He knew what had happened on the common, and running away was worse for him than it was for me, since he was a man grown.

"We're going to fight them today, Adam," he said to me.

"I know."

"Things happen in fighting."

"Yes, sir. I guess the most terrible and unexpected things happen."

"I pray to God to spare us both, Adam."

"Amen to that."

"But no one knows. As Jehovah wills it, so it will be, but if anything does happen, I want you to tell it to Ruth, and be kind and considerate of her, Adam. A girl is a frail thing, and not easy in the world until she has a home and a family of her own."

I promised him, even though I couldn't think of Ruth Simmons as a frail thing. She was one of the strongest and healthiest girls in our town.

We heard gunfire. It was distant and faint and in the direction of Concord, but it brought everyone in the pasture to his feet, and we stood there listening and staring. Then a rider came across the fields, spurring his horse, sailing over a stone wall, and pulling up hard and sharp at the pasture, with everybody crowding around him to hear the news that he brought. Church bells were ringing again. It was hard to say exactly where the bells were, but you could hear them from the south and from the west.

The rider brought news that the British army was in Concord. Most everything had been taken away from there and hidden, only some hogsheads of wheat flour left. Who would have dreamed that the redcoats would smash them up and strew the flour all over the place, but according to the rider, that was exactly what they had done. The redcoat officers were sitting outside of the inn, drinking everything and paying for nothing, and making a great picnic out of the whole thing. There were no men to speak of left in Concord, only women and children.

"But the gunfire?" demanded Solomon Chandler. "What of the gunfire, man?"

The rider didn't know. He had only heard the gunfire as he approached us. But he did know that there had been talk among the British of destroying the North Bridge. And the militia were on the west bank of the river. There might have been a fight at the river.

There was more gunfire while we questioned him, scattered bursts, and then single shots popping lightly, so faint it was hardly possible to define them with any certainty.

"Well, what are their plans? Do they leave Concord?"

He didn't know. He pleaded his thirst, and someone handed him a water bottle. The day was turning hot and preparing to be the hottest day of the year until then.

"Do you have the nerve to go back there?" he was asked.

He did. He nodded his head vigorously. His horse was a beautiful chestnut gelding. He was about nineteen years old, and proud of his riding. He said that if it had to be, he'd ride through the redcoat army.

"Never you mind such tricks."

Well, what did we want him to do?

"Go back and listen for when they march."

"And then?"

"Cut into the road and ride down before them, yelling an alarm. You're a young man. You got a good set of lungs."

"Well, don't shoot at me by mistake."

"Go on with you!"

He rode away, waving back at us.

Solomon Chandler stood up on the stone wall, and the men gathered around. I didn't count them then, but I am sure there were well over a hundred in the pasture. One man had two hunting dogs with him.

"Send the dogs home, neighbor," Chandler said. "There's no need to flush what we hunt." It raised a laugh, and I could see how much they enjoyed the old man. He stood up on the stone wall, tall and skinny as a fence rail, his hands in his pocket, his long rifle slung over his back, his pipe in his mouth. Then he tapped out his pipe on the back of one hand, and said:

"Well, here we are, neighbors, and who ever would have thought it would come to fighting on a fine Middlesex morning like this one? But it has. It has. The redcoats danced, didn't they, and now they got to pay the piper. It wouldn't be at all proper to let them go home and exact no payment. I know that the Reverend could say all and more that must be said, and when he does, I do hope that he will turn to Exodus 21, for it is written there, 'He that smiteth a man, so that he die, shall be surely put to death. And if a man lie not in wait, but God deliver him into his hand; then I will appoint thee a place whither he shall flee. But if a man come presumptuously upon his neighbor, to slay him with guile; thou shalt take him from mine altar, that he may die.' "

"Amen!" came up from the pasture.

"Amen. Now how many of you are riflemen, raise your weapons!"

About twenty men raised rifles, holding them up over their heads for Solomon Chandler to see.

"Good!" the old man said. "Go over to my left and separate yourselves, and I'll be captain with you, and Joshua Dover with the muskets and bird guns. Unless anyone wants to propose it differently. If they do, I'm willing to hear."

"Why can't we stay together, Solomon?"

"You answer that, son. A musket gun carries a hundred paces. A rifle carries four hundred paces. That calls for two different kinds of tactics entirely. Now just let me explain what I have in mind. Consider the five miles of road between here and Lexington. It seems plain to me that the redcoats are going to march down that stretch of road. It would be five miles more by way of Lincoln to Watertown, and no sense whatsoever, so it's safe to presume they'll take the road to the north of us. All that five miles to Lexington, and ten miles more to Charlestown, we'll give them no peace whatsoever. At least half the stretch of that road is binded with stone wall. We'll lie down behind that wall and make them mighty uncomfortable."

I wondered. Could you be shot down and run away in such fear as we had on the common, and then fight and win—and all of it on the same day? It was one thing to see the redcoats in the distance, and something else to have them close up against you. If someone had to tell them, I was still not the one. I went with Cousin Simmons in the file of men walking toward the road, and it didn't seem possible that we were at war, not even with the shots popping like Indian corn in the distance. The Reverend was with us. He had a gun now, a bag of shot, and a bottle of powder, and under the day's growth of whiskers his face was sad and lonely. Solomon Chandler came over to wish me Godspeed.

"Prime your gun careful, and don't ever fire unless the man's upon you. Count his buttons. A gun like yours won't stop a man at more than thirty paces."

"Yes, sir," I said. "I'll heed your words."

"Take no pleasure in it. Let it hurt, but become hard in the sorrow."

"Would you tell him that?" the Reverend asked.

"And you, too, Reverend. I tell you that. We'll weep for them, but they brought the killing to us, not us to them."

"God help all of us," the Reverend said.

"I say amen to that. We fight in God's cause."

"Nobody fights in God's cause," the Reverend replied harshly. "Isn't it enough to kill in freedom's name? No one kills in God's cause. He can only ask God's forgiveness."

The old man heard this respectfully. "As you

say, Reverend. I would like to dispute it somewhat, but there ain't time." Then he turned off
with his riflemen to find a hummock overlooking
the road, while we filed through a scrub of woods
to the stone wall that lined the road. We took
our places on the blind side of the wall, a man of
us every few yards, stretching down along the
road to where it curved out of sight, and with
the road itself not ten paces from where we were.

"We'll keep down after we shoot," Cousin
Simmons said, "and get out. Then we can take
other places down the road. It's just death to
try to remain here with the roadway full of
British regulars." Most everyone agreed with
him, and when Cousin Joshua came down the
wall to check our positions, he said the same
thing.

"How long to wait, Joshua?" the Reverend
asked him. The Reverend was on one side of me,
Cousin Simmons on the other.

"I hear the shooting plainer, don't you?"

We were sitting on top of the wall; it was
strange to see the men sitting there, as far as the
wall stretched, and I couldn't remember anything
like it that I had ever seen before.

"Plainer, I think."

It was so. The pop, pop, pop of gunfire was
becoming louder. It no longer sounded like Indian corn. My heart began to hammer wildly, and
suddenly I felt that I would burst if I didn't pass
water.

"Do it here," Cousin Simmons said.

"Can't with the Reverend watching."

"Don't be a fool, boy. Don't you think the
Reverend does the same thing? He'll be doing it
enough before the day's through."

"Go ahead and put modesty away, Adam," the Reverend agreed.

I did it. It was woefully hot, the sweat pouring down my face, and Cousin Simmons said why didn't I take off my coat. I replied that I couldn't, because I might lose it in the excitement, and it was the very best jacket coat I ever owned and brand new in the bargain. "And you wore it last night!" Cousin Simmons cried. The Reverend burst into laughter. It was the first time any of us had laughed since the morning began.

The rider from Concord was as good as his word. He came spurring and whooping down the road, his horse kicking up clouds of dust, shouting:

"They're a-coming! By God, they're a-coming, they are!"

We heard him before he ever showed, and we heard him yelling after he was out of sight. Solomon Chandler hadn't misjudged the strength of his lungs, not at all. I think you could have heard him a mile away, and he was bursting at every seam with importance. I have observed that being up on a horse changes the whole character of a man, and when a very small man is up on a saddle, he'd like as not prefer to eat his meals there. That's understandable, and I appreciate the sentiment. As for this rider, I never saw him before or afterwards and never saw him dismounted, so whether he stood tall or short in his shoes, I can't say; but I do know that he gave the day tone and distinction. The last thing in the world that resembled a war was our line of farmers and storekeepers and mechanics perched on top of a stone wall, and this dashing rider made us feel a good deal sharper and more alert to the situation.

We came down off the wall as if he had toppled all of us, and we crouched behind it. I have heard people talk with contempt about the British regulars, but that only proves that a lot of people talk about things of which they are deplorably ignorant. Whatever we felt about the redcoats, we respected them in terms of their trade, which was killing; and I know that I, myself, was nauseated with apprehension and fear and that my hands were soaking wet where they held my gun. I wanted to wipe my flint, but I didn't dare to, the state my hands were in, just as I didn't dare to do anything about the priming. The gun would fire or not, just as chance willed. I put a lot more trust in my two legs than in the gun, because the most important thing I had learned about war was that you could run away and survive to talk about it.

The gunfire, which was so near that it seemed just a piece up the road now, stopped for long enough to count to twenty; and in that brief interval, a redcoat officer came tearing down the road, whipping his horse fit to kill. I don't know whether he was after our rider, who had gone by a minute before, or whether he was simply scouting conditions; but when he passed us by, a musket roared, and he reared his horse, swung it around, and began to whip it back in the direction from which he had come. He was a fine and showy rider, but his skill was wasted on us. From above me and somewhere behind me, a rifle cracked. The redcoat officer collapsed like a punctured bolster, and the horse reared and threw him from the saddle, except that one booted foot caught in the stirrup. Half crazed by the weight dragging, the dust, and the heat, the horse leaped our wall, dashing out the rider's brains against it, and leaving him lying there among us—while the horse crashed away through the brush.

It was my initiation to war and the insane symphony war plays; for what had happened on the common was only terror and flight; but this grinning, broken head, not ten feet away from me, was the sharp definition of what my reality had become.

And now the redcoats were coming, and the gunfire was a part of the dust cloud on the road to the west of us. I must state that the faster things happened, the slower they happened, the passage and rhythm of time changed, and when I remember back to what happened then, each event is a separate and frozen incident. In my recollection, there was a long interval between the death of the officer and the appearance of the first of the retreating redcoats, and in that interval the dust cloud over the road seems to hover indefinitely. Yet it could not have been more than a matter of seconds, and then the front of the British army came into view.

It was only hours since I had last seen them, but they had changed and I had changed. In the very front rank, two men were wounded and staggered along, trailing blood behind them. No drummers here, no pipers, and the red coats were covered with a fine film of dust. They marched with bayonets fixed, and as fixed on their faces was anger, fear, and torment. Rank after rank of them came down the road, and the faces were all the same, and they walked in a sea of dust.

"Committeemen, hold your fire!" a voice called, and what made it even more terrible and unreal was that the redcoat ranks never paused for an instant, only some of them glancing toward the stone wall, from behind which the voice came.

The front of their column had already passed us, when another officer came riding down the side of the road, not five paces from where we were. My Cousin Simmons carried a musket, but he had loaded it with bird shot, and as the officer came opposite him, he rose up behind the wall and fired. One moment there was a man in the saddle; the next a headless horror on a horse that bolted through the redcoat ranks, and during the next second or two, we all of us fired into the suddenly disorganized column of soldiers. One moment, the road was filled with disciplined troops, marching four by four with a purpose as implacable as death; the next, a cloud of gun smoke covered a screaming fury of sound, out of which the redcoat soldiers emerged with their bayonets and their cursing fury.

In the course of this, they had fired on us; but I have no memory of that. I had squeezed the trigger of my own gun, and to my amazement, it had fired and kicked back into my shoulder with the force of an angry mule; and then I was adding my own voice to the crescendo of sound, hurling more vile language than I ever thought I knew, sobbing and shouting, and aware that if I had passed water before, it was not enough, for my pants were soaking wet.

I would have stood there and died there if left to myself, but Cousin Simmons grabbed my arm in his viselike grip and fairly plucked me out of there; and then I came to some sanity and plunged away with such extraordinary speed that I outdistanced Cousin Simmons by far. Everyone else was running. Later we realized that the redcoats had stopped their charge at the wall. Their only hope of survival was to hold to the road and keep marching.

We tumbled to a stop in Deacon Gordon's cow hole, a lowlying bit of pasture with a muddy pool of water in its middle. A dozen cows mooed sadly and regarded us as if we were insane, as perhaps we were at that moment, with the crazy excitement of our first encounter, the yelling and shooting still continuing up at the road, and the thirst of some of the men, which was so great that they waded into the muddy water and scooped up handfuls of it. Isaac Pitt, one of the men from Lincoln, had taken a musket ball in his belly; and though he had found the strength to run with us, now he collapsed and lay on the ground, dying, the Reverend holding his head and wiping his hot brow. It may appear that we were cruel and callous, but no one had time to spend sympathizing with poor Isaac—except the Reverend. I know that I myself felt that it was a mortal shame for a man to be torn open by a British musket ball, as Isaac had been, yet I also felt relieved and lucky that it had been him and not myself. I was drunk with excitement and the smell of gunpowder that came floating down from the road, and the fact that I was not afraid now, but only waiting to know what to do next.

Meanwhile, I reloaded my gun, as the other men were doing. We were less than a quarter of a mile from the road, and we could trace its shape from the ribbon of powder smoke and dust that hung over it. Wherever you looked, you saw Committeemen running across the meadows, some away from the road, some toward it, some parallel to it; and about a mile to the west a cluster of at least fifty militia were making their way in our direction.

Cousin Joshua and some others felt that we should march toward Lexington and take up new positions ahead of the slow-moving British column, but another group maintained that we should stick to this spot and this section of road. I didn't offer any advice, but I certainly did not want to go back to where the officer lay with his brains dashed out. Someone said that while we were standing here and arguing about it, the British would be gone; but Cousin Simmons said he had watched them marching west early in the morning, and moving at a much brisker pace it had still taken half an hour for their column to pass, what with the narrowness of the road and their baggage and ammunition carts.

While this was being discussed, we saw the militia to the west of us fanning out and breaking into little clusters of two and three men as they approached the road. It was the opinion of some of us that these must be part of the Committeemen who had been in the Battle of the North Bridge, which entitled them to a sort of veteran status, and we felt that if they employed this tactic, it was likely enough the best one. Mattathias Dover said:

"It makes sense. If we cluster together, the redcoats can make an advantage out of it, but there's not a blessed thing they can do with two or three of us except chase us, and we can outrun them."

That settled it, and we broke into parties of two and three. Cousin Joshua Dover decided to remain with the Reverend and poor Isaac Pitt until life passed away—and he was hurt so badly he did not seem for long in this world. I went off with Cousin Simmons, who maintained that if he didn't see to me, he didn't know who would.

"Good heavens, Adam," he said, "I thought one thing you'd have no trouble learning is when to get out of a place."

"I learned that now," I said.

We ran east for about half a mile before we turned back to the road, panting from the effort and soaked with sweat. There was a clump of trees that appeared to provide cover right up to the road, and the shouting and gunfire never slackened.

Under the trees, there was a dead redcoat, a young boy with a pasty white skin and a face full of pimples, who had taken a rifle ball directly between the eyes. Three men were around him. They had stripped him of his musket and equipment, and now they were pulling his boots and jacket off. Cousin Simmons grabbed one of them by the shoulder and flung him away.

"God's name, what are you to rob the dead with the fight going on!" Cousin Simmons roared.

They tried to outface him, but Joseph Simmons was as wide as two average men, and it would have taken braver men than these were to outface him. They blustered, and then took off, and I asked Cousin Simmons who he thought they were.

"Never saw them before. I tell you they're no Committeemen, I tell you that, Adam. Most likely, they're Boston men, the way they behave." He didn't think highly of Boston men, for reasons I went into earlier.

I couldn't help looking again and again at the face of the dead redcoat. What struck me hardest was how small he was. Perhaps it was his position in death, but he appeared no taller than my brother, Levi, and his purple lips were drawn back from a mouth half toothless. His blue eyes were wide open, and his face was so thin and pinched and starved that I became sick all over again, and wept as I vomited. Cousin Simmons pulled me away, and then as we approached the road, he got down on his knees and crawled. I did as he did, and soon we were in a space between two rocks, with the road a bit beneath us and some fifty paces away.

There was no powder smoke here now, but westward, where the road ran through a dip, there was a great deal of firing and a whole cloud of smoke. Here, the redcoats were plainly visible as they trudged by, their faces grim and murderous, their scarlet coats no longer bright. Two dead redcoats lay on the edge of the road, on the side away from us. Four others, who were wounded, sat alongside the dead. As they marched, a cart drawn by a brace of mules appeared in the column. The soldiers continued to march, crowding around the cart, while it was loaded with the dead and the wounded. There must have been half a dozen dead bodies already in the cart, and two wounded men shared the space with them. Now two more dead and four more wounded filled the cart to overflowing. We could hear the wounded moaning and cursing in their pain as the cart went by, and Cousin Simmons whispered that war was a dirty and terrible business.

"We don't know any of them," I whispered back. "They're strangers here in our land. We don't know who that boy back there is. We'll never know his name, no one will."

"We got to make war on them, Adam."

"Then let's shoot. I can't stay here like this."

His hand gripped my shoulder. "Easy," he whispered. "Now—one, two—" And then we both fired. A redcoat flung out his hands and fell. Two others yelled in pain from my bird shot, and then the whole column was screaming curses in our direction and loosing a volley of musket fire. We lay pressed to the ground as the balls whined overhead and buried themselves in the trees; and then we leaped up and got out of there, racing through the woods, leaping a stone wall, and then panting and listening to the cursing rage and the constant sound of gunfire.

"Water, please," I begged Cousin Simmons.

He handed me his bottle and said, "Finish it, Adam. Then we can get water at the Atkins place, over yonder."

I drained the whole bottle, stared for a moment at Cousin Simmons, and then said, "No more. Isn't it enough?"

"That's not for me to say, Adam. Listen to the gunfire. That's our flesh and blood fighting there. Can you walk away from them?"

"Will it bring my father back?"

"No, Adam. Nothing will bring him back. But we're not fighting an eye for an eye and a tooth for a tooth. That's how old Solomon Chandler sees it, but the Scripture is not meant to be taken literally, as some would have it. This is a war, Adam."

"Why? Why?"

"A man's land is his own, Adam. A man's place is his own. All we wished when we stood out on the common was to tell them that this was our place. We had no riches or gold or silver. Your father would have said to them, Go home and leave us be. This is our place, our common, our meeting house, and our houses. We are a Committee to defend what is ours. There will be trouble if you march into our land and work your will on us. That's all he wanted to say to them, but they chose to have it differently, and now it's too late. The war is all over us."

He rose and pointed southward, where a broad wheat field sloped up to the horizon. Men were coming across it. The word went out, and the sound of shots carried farther than you could hear them, and all morning the men had been coming, and still they were coming as the news was passed on.

We went on to the Atkins place. They had a barn that was less than a quarter of a mile from the road, and on the peaked roof of the barn four riflemen stood, firing as carefully as if they were on a turkey range. Solomon Chandler was one of them, but I no longer felt any warmth toward the old man. I would kill and he would kill, but he took pleasure in the killing. Cold as ice, he stood up there on the roof and picked his targets from the smoky road. He waved to me and shouted:

"I got me a redcoat officer, laddie boy. There he was up on the road on his prancing horse. Three hundred paces, and I picked him off neat as a feather. The hand of Jehovah reached down and smote him."

Another man joined us below and called up to them, "Can you see the whole redcoat army?"

"Where there ain't smoke, you can see it. But it ain't the whole redcoat army! Oh, no! Not by a bushel or two, no, sir!"

As a matter of fact, the road was defined by the powder smoke that lay over it. The noonday sun was overhead, and it was a windless, unseasonably hot day. Some of the smoke drifted and dissipated, but most of it hung over the road like a thick curtain—a fact that the redcoats should have thanked God for, since without the smoke to cover them, it is questionable whether a man of them would have gotten through. We learned later that the British commander was ready to surrender his army at this point, but there was no one to surrender to; and often enough, lying sleepless at night, I imagined how that march must have been for the redcoats, trudging down that burning road, the dust and the powder smoke choking them, a pale sun burning through, and the Middlesex men hidden behind stones and walls and trees.

The firing never stopped. It blazed up at one point and then at another. About thirty men had gathered at the Atkins place, and we went up to the road to fire a volley into it. Then we went back to the well, where the Atkins women were drawing water. All our fear of the redcoats had vanished, and somehow we knew as certainly as if they had signed a paper to such effect that they would not break their march and leave the road. Yet perhaps not all our fear—for there was one thing we did not do, and that was to block-ade the road and stop them. It was one thing to fight them as we were fighting them; something else to stand up to their muskets without cover.

Mrs. Atkins and her daughter Esther and her twelve-year-old son Ishmael were all drawing water and working at the well fit to break their backs. They were good-hearted people, the women a little subdued by the number of menfolk in their family and a good deal bewildered by the fact that a part of a war was being fought a quarter of a mile away. Aside from being thoughtfully placed along the British line of march, their well was a deep one, with a considerable reputation for cold and pure water. When we got there, Cousin Simmons couldn't bear to watch those women breaking their backs over the well handle. He said he didn't think that war was any reason for men to turn into hogs and women into slaves; and he took over the handle himself and then shamed some others into turns. Those women had raised fifty buckets out of the well already, and anyone who ever turned a well handle knows what that means.

Myself, I must have drunk half a bucket of ice-cold water sweet as honey, and some more to pour over my aching head. The Atkins women had brought out every scrap of bread and provision in their house, and no one went away from there hungry. I was wolfing down some sausage and bread, when Esther Atkins came over to me and asked whether I wasn't the Cooper boy from Lexington.

I said I was. She was a handsome girl of seventeen or so, with black eyes and black hair, and it was said that she had more suitors than a dog has fleas.

"But last time I saw you, you were just a shaver."

"I'm fifteen, ma'am."

"I heard tell about your father. Moses Cooper. He was your father?"

"Yes, he was."

"I'm sorry—oh, indeed, I am."

One of her own brothers would be dead before the day was finished, but neither of us knew that then, and she brought me a piece of berry pie out of the kindness of wanting to do for me. Many people were kind and gentle on that day; it

wasn't unrelieved horror, and fewer were cruel
than you might have thought. I saw at least
three men carrying wounded neighbors on their
backs, and there was another incident as we
moved eastward that was worth remembering.

You see, about thirty men had gathered at
the Atkins place. Some of them were Lincoln
Town men, who had come up with Cousin Joshua
Dover, and others were from the neighborhood
and from across the Sudbury River. Two of these
were in the fight at the North Bridge, where
Yankees of Massachusetts fired upon the British
for the first time, although they held, as we did,
that not a man among them fired his weapon
until the redcoats had loosed a volley and slain
two good Concord men and wounded others. The
leader of the Sudbury men was one Alan Becket, a
small, nervous, energetic man who complained bitterly that the battle was being fought without
rhyme or reason, that nothing had really been
planned, and that for all our cutting and sniping
at the British, we were letting a whole army of
them escape, when here was a golden opportunity
either for capturing them or wiping them out to
the last man.

For my own part, I was ready to live and let
live. I was beginning to react to the sleepless
night, and every bone and muscle in my body felt
my fatigue. It had appeared to me, from all I had
ever read or heard about war, that a battle was
fought quickly and then put away to rest and
wait for inclusion in the history books; and I felt
that I had been through three battles already,
and it was enough. But Becket held otherwise,
and he was persuasive enough to bring the men
around to his way of thinking.

He said that instead of running back and forth to the road to take pot shots at the redcoats, and wearing ourselves out in the process, we should head southeast and pick up the Menotomy Road south of Lexington, about five miles from where we now were. Even without hurrying, we could reach that spot before the British did, and as we moved we could gather to us all the Committeemen we encountered. With even a hundred men, we could try to trap the British somewhere between Lexington and Menotomy, and if we could hold them up for an hour or two, we might find that several thousand Committeemen had arrived to join us.

It all seemed very iffish and offhand to me, but Cousin Simmons agreed that it was at least a plan of a sort, and that was better than just milling around with no plan at all, with everyone a commander and everyone changing his mind. By now, Solomon Chandler and the other riflemen had come down from the barn roof, and they gave their support to Becket's plan. The last stragglers of the redcoat army had passed by the point of road opposite us, and while we could overtake them easily enough, Chandler was of the opinion that it made far more sense to try to cut them off south of Lexington. More men were joining us, and when we began to march, we numbered better than half a hundred.

We were almost a mile south of the Concord Road when we crossed the Lincoln Road, fifteen or twenty minutes later, and just as we were crossing it, as luck would have it, a redcoat cavalry patrol came down from the north, perhaps scouting to see whether the road to Lincoln might offer an alternative route of escape. There were four men in the patrol, and as they came into sight, at least twenty of us fired at them. Three of them whipped their horses around and got away, but the fourth fell out of his saddle and lay in the road, his horse standing beside him. It was poor shooting, but I had discovered that it was always poor shooting when men let off their pieces in a hurry, never stopping to consider or take reasonable aim. It was a condition I was grateful for, since it kept a good many folks alive who would otherwise be dead.

We rushed over to the fallen man and crowded around him—not yet being enough of soldiers to suspect the possibility of a larger force returning —and we saw that he was conscious, with a bullet hole in his shoulder. He was a pink-cheeked boy of about twenty, and after he had looked at us, he closed his eyes and prepared to be shot to death by the barbarians we had been described to him as being. But his courage wasn't sufficient to prevent tears of pain and fear from rolling down his dirty cheeks; and the sight of him lying there and crying and looking so much like a little boy had its effect on all of us. I know that I had a hard time to keep from crying myself.

Dr. Cody of Watertown was with us, and although our family had always regarded him as a fraud and a quack, he did a quick and handy job of stopping the bleeding and tying up the wound. Then we picked up the boy and carried him all the way to the Dunn House, where we left him.

Some of the men wanted Becket to ride his horse. I respected Becket for saying that he would feel foolish up there, and anyway he deferred to Solomon Chandler's age. Chandler was pleased as a boy at riding the British filly, his rifle dangling forward like an old-time lance.

Cousin Simmons remarked that there was

nothing to bring out a man's innermost character like being up on a horse while everyone else walked along on the two feet God gave him.

# The Afternoon

We were about a mile and a half to the south of Lexington now, between the Watertown Road and the Menotomy Road; and all that was home to me, all that was warm and sweet and good, my mother and my brother Levi and Granny and Ruth, my relatives and my friends—all of this was a hoot and a holler away, just over the hill and across the trees, just so near that I could almost reach out and touch it; but instead of going home, as any sane person would, I was part of a motley group of farmers who were off to trap a British army and destroy it. It made no sense whatsoever, and I said so to Cousin Simmons.

"Well, Adam," he said, scratching his head, "it's war now, you know, and in wartime things don't make sense the way they would in peacetime."

"I had a belly full of war and killing, Cousin Simmons."

"I know that, Adam. So have I, when you come right down to it. Maybe so has everybody here except an old fire-eater like Solomon Chandler. But we can't stop."

"Why not?"

"Good heavens, Adam, we declared ourselves. There just is no stronger declaration of a man's purpose than to take a gun and shoot someone dead."

"But they shot us first."

"That's an argument, Adam, and we're past arguments. Gun shooting is a declaration, not an argument. Nobody's going to be calm and reason-

159

able about who shot first. There's been too much shooting already to ever trace our way back. Now we're enemies until one side or another wins its purpose. If we were to back off now they'd come with their gallows rope and hang up maybe a hundred, maybe a thousand, maybe ten thousand. We'd never sleep a peaceful night again—not ever again, no sir."

"Then when will it end?"

"When will it end, Adam? I'll tell you when it will end—when we drive them back into their ships, and when their ships sail away from here and leave us in peace in our own land. Not until then."

"You're talking about a time. Maybe years of time," I said wearily.

"Maybe years of time, Adam. That's true."

"I'm talking about today, Cousin Simmons. I'm talking about right now—about going home right now."

"Heavens to Holland, lad—where would you go? The redcoats are no doubt entering Lexington right this precious minute."

"They wouldn't catch me."

"There's a real smart observation. Suppose you tell me how you are going to manage that."

"I'd crawl up," I muttered. "I'd lay there at the edge of town until they left."

"Why, the place is crawling with them—and you'd go crawling in there? That makes no sense at all, Adam, and you know it."

"Maybe I do know it, Cousin Simmons. I'm just sick of this whole bloody business."

"I can understand that," Cousin Simmons nodded. "You're just a boy, Adam, and you've had a hard enough time of it and a long day to boot, a terrible long day. Don't you think I'd like to see you out of this, you being my own kin and father-less? But that's just it."

"What is?"

"The fact that you're Moses Cooper's first-born and there isn't a man here doesn't know it — and doesn't know he was killed in the slaughter."

We paused for a few minutes to rest ourselves on the little bare hillock we called the Indian burying ground—although so far as I knew, no one was buried there. My father once told me that the Indians, being heathen, did not properly bury their dead, but built a sort of frame structure on the burying ground and laid their dead upon it, open and uncovered to the sky and the sun and the rain and the snow. I had liked the notion and half-regretted that I was not born an Indian; for it seemed infinitely preferable to being lowered into a deep, wet hole in the ground. Now the thought came back to me, a stabbing awakening of grief and remorse—the guilt attached to the way I had allowed myself to be flung into the battle and absorbed by it, with my father lying in our home, hardly even cold with death. I felt that the least I could do for him was to keep my thoughts on him and keep my sorrow alive.

I felt even worse when someone shouted that Lexington was burning. There were well over a hundred and fifty men in our little army by now, and we all stood dumfounded and helpless on the little hillock, staring northward where smoke rose into the sky. We discovered subsequently that only three houses had been set afire and actually burned down, the Loring House, the Mullikan House and the Bond House; but from the amount of smoke in the sky, it appeared to us then that the entire village was being consumed. I was sick at heart with the thought that our house was burning, and that there was nothing at all that I could do about it. I was asking myself, What about Mother and Granny and Levi? Were they in the house? For all I knew, they could be hiding down in the cellar, trapped there, with the house burning down over their heads. I said as much to Cousin Simmons, whose own face was desolate enough.

"Oh, no, Adam," he replied sadly. "That's one thing you don't have to worry about. Your grandmother would not hide herself in the cellar if all the dragoons in England were in her front yard. It's Ruthie and Goody Simmons I'm distressed about. It's a bitter thing for a man to have to stand idle and helpless and watch his home being consumed into ashes."

Some of the men began to talk of going up and attacking the British and driving them out of the town. It was wild, desperate talk. We had inflicted awful damage upon the redcoats and and would do more before the day was over—but not by going up against the volleys of their muskets when they could all stand in their lines together and see what they were shooting at. So the talk was only talk—no more than that. Jonathan Crisp, who had been on the common with us, was there, with his cousin Salem, who was a year younger than he; and they both burst into tears. The men watched them, and shook their heads sadly, because the whole world appeared to be crumbling around us; and none of us had been prepared for it or had anticipated it. It had happened too quickly. I could see that the men were driving themselves sick with their frustration—such a crowd of us standing here on the hillock and not being able to do one blessed thing to rescue the town from the redcoats.

Then Solomon Chandler sang out, so that everyone would hear him, "One thing, lads, the British are there now—but not for long! The last of them will be out before the hour's up!"

"Why?"

"Because it makes sense. Either they're back in Boston by darkness or they'll never be back there again!"

The men let out a cheer to that. Everyone wanted to find a reason to extract a crumb of comfort. And just then, three Committeemen on horseback came riding up. They had a force of a hundred men from Watertown and Cambridge, and they were waiting down along the Menotomy Road. Just about a mile from where we were. They told us that a relief army of redcoats from Boston, fifteen hundred of them, had gone by about an hour ago into Lexington, and that before another hour was up they'd probably all be marching down the road and back to Boston. They were out to find everyone they could, so that the redcoats would retain a good and substantial memory of the Menotomy Road.

"And you found us, you did," Solomon Chandler grinned.

That broke the tension. Everyone began to talk and shout and swear and wave their guns. It was a wild mood that took hold of the men, as if they realized, as Cousin Simmons had put it, that there was no more undoing of what had been done.

Solomon Chandler climbed onto his horse and shouted, "Follow me, laddies!" and then we all streamed after him, down off the hillock and toward the Menotomy Road. I didn't want to go, yet I went. We all went. We were in the grip of a force outside of ourselves. I know that my heart was breaking with anxiety over the burning of the village, and I tried to give myself strength and purpose by telling myself that everything that I had ever loved was destroyed or dead, and I might as well be dead too.

There was a place our people had in mind where the Menotomy Road dips between two banks of earth, with a great tangle of wild blackberry bushes on one side and a windfall of dead trees on the other. I knew the place well, because the bramble patch made for the best rabbit hunting in the whole neighborhood, and many was the time Father and I hiked down there for an early morning's shooting. Now the plan was to drag enough fallen trees across the road to block it, and then back the trees up with rocks and dirt. With such a breastwork, we felt we could hold the British long enough for a considerable army of Essex men, who were said to be marching in under the leadership of Colonel Pickering, to reach us. I suppose that there was some vague possibility that the plan might have worked; in any case, it was the only plan of any sort that emerged from that incredible and catch-as-catch-can day of battle. Everything else that happened was the result of some sudden notion of this or that Committeeman; and the only reason that the battle went on hour after hour was that no one was in any position to halt it or direct it. It was perfectly true that before the reinforcements reached the first redcoat army, they wanted to surrender. They were just about going out of their minds, plagued by an enemy they couldn't see, unable to use any tactics of battle they had learned or practiced in Europe, shooting away all their ammunition at stone walls, woods, and thickets, and losing almost a quarter of their number in dead and wounded. But there was no one they could surrender to, no one they could talk to or parley with; and when one of them came to the roadside west of Lexington with a white flag, he was shot dead by Abraham Clyde of Concord, who thought the white flag was only another one of the various regimental flags the redcoats carried.

So our plan might have worked and everything that followed might have been different, if the British hadn't already started down the Menotomy Road before we reached it. We were still a quarter of a mile away when we heard the Watertown and Cambridge men banging away at them.

Cousin Simmons and I and four or five of the others crawled into the windfall, and wriggled our way through the tangle of trees until we got a view of a few yards of the road. We were as well hidden there as a fox in her earth, about sixty or seventy paces from the road, and we began to shoot at the redcoats passing by. It was a strange and dreamlike business, lying there and seeing bits of red color emerge from the powder smoke that hung all over the place and over the road as well, then watching everything disappear under the smoke and only the smoke to shoot into, and then a bit of red here or a bit of red there—and such a feeling of a world gone mad, for there was nothing the redcoats could do but march on and accept their measure of death—and the bulk of our Committeemen running down the road from place to place, so that they were always with the army, like flies on a dying beast.

But we, our little group of people, remained

in our cover—for there was no way that the redcoats could reach us, and most of us were too
tired now to go on running back and forth along
the road. We lay there and fired at the redcoats
and the smoke; or at least Cousin Simmons and
the others did; I fired off my fowling piece once,
and then I realized that at this range, even if
some of the bird shot did reach the redcoats, it
would sting no harder than a mosquito. It was a
great relief to find some sensible reason not to go
on shooting. I burrowed into the ground behind a
fallen tree, rested my cheek against the stock of
my gun, listened to the shooting and screaming
and cursing—more profanity in five minutes than
one heard in our village in the course of a year—
and then fell asleep.

It might strike you as strange that I could
fall asleep right in the midst of a battle; and you
might even consider it downright ungracious that
anyone should go to sleep during a battle as
talked about and lied about and written about
as this one; but the fact of the matter was that
I had gone without a night's sleep, and been
through the massacre on the common, and had
quartered back and forth across the country since
then like a fox driven to distraction—so that the
wonder of it was, not that I had finally fallen
asleep, but that I had managed to remain awake
as long as this.

I was awakened by the silence. I guess it was
the first silence in six or seven hours, and it was
just unbelievable and a little frightening as well.

I don't mean that it was a complete and total
silence, or anything unnatural or spooky. There
were sounds in the distance and in the back-

ground, as there always are, but even these sounds were muffled by the tangled pile of trees; and missing were the violent and awful sounds of battle, the crash of firearms and the savage shouting and swearing of men in anger and pain. When I listened more carefully, I thought I could still hear battle sounds, but far off and very faint. It was still daylight outside, but under the windfall was a sort of comforting twilight, and being used to gauging time without a pocket watch, I had a feeling that at least an hour had passed.

I lay still for a little while after I awakened, luxuriating in the peace, and then I heard the noise of twigs and branches breaking, men making their way into the windfall, and voices; first the voice of the Reverend:

"God be kind to us, Joseph, and merciful. I tell you frankly that I don't have the courage to go back to Goody Cooper and tell her that her son as well as her husband lies dead today."

"What about myself?" Cousin Simmons answered him. "Aside from having the boy's blood on my own conscience, I'll have to face her. Why didn't you send him home? she'll ask me."

"The boy's blood isn't on your conscience, Joseph. No man's blood is on anyone's conscience today—unless it be on the conscience of the Englishmen who made the first slaughter on the common."

"You don't know Goody Cooper, Reverend."

"Where did you see him last? Where did you leave him?"

"Trouble is, Reverend, I don't think I ever knew a better or more uncomplaining boy."

"He was a good boy, Joseph. No question about that."

"It just shakes my faith in the Almighty to think of the innocent cut down like this."

"Nothing should shake your faith, Joseph. His ways are inscrutable."

"Uncomplaining, Reverend. When you consider all that boy went through since last night—"

At first, it was pleasant and rewarding to lie there and listen to them talk about me in the past tense. I guess there never was a boy who didn't imagine himself dead, so that he could take comfort out of the fine things said about him. But there was a note in their voices that made me wonder whether they had the same respect for my intelligence as for my forbearance. I sat up and called out to them.

"God be praised!" the Reverend cried.

Helping me to my feet, Cousin Simmons asked if I was wounded.

"No, sir, I'm all right."

"Then what on earth happened to you, Adam?"

"I fell asleep."

The both of them stared at me open-mouthed. "You what?"

"I fell asleep," I repeated. "I just fell asleep."

"So long as you're all right," the Reverend said.

They helped me out of the windfall, and I asked Cousin Simmons about the battle.

"It's down past Cambridge by now, and the Committeemen are marching in from all over. If the redcoats get back to Boston, they're there to stay. There'll be five thousand of our men around Boston before nightfall."

"Then can we go home?" I asked him.

"We're all going home, Adam—there's others had more sleep and more rest."

But what I would be coming home to I didn't know; and for all I knew, the town could be in ashes and everyone dear to me, dead.

When I saw the tower of the meetinghouse, I felt better, and then I saw the Parker barns on the outskirts of town, and I told myself that if they had burned one, they would have burned the other too. You might think we would run in our haste to be there and see what had happened, but you don't hurry for bad news. Also, we were tired, all three of us. So we came up to the town slowly, and bit by bit we realized that it still stood, only the three houses that I spoke of before burned down.

I left Cousin Simmons and the Reverend to go to my own house. We were not the only ones returning to the village. Others came across the fields, and still others were trudging wearily up the Menotomy Road—and all of them could be defined by a sort of tired sadness that was evident in the way they walked and the way they trailed their guns. We had won the battle, but there is less joy in winning a battle than the history books tell you.

"Best to go home, Adam," the Reverend said. "I will come by and pay my respects later."

I would have begged them to come along with me and not leave me with the task of facing what awaited me alone, but when I looked at them, I had no heart to. Both of them had aged woefully. Their faces were gray and drawn, covered with a stubble of beard, with dirt and grime and dried blood. Their clothes were torn and filthy, and their eyes were red with fatigue and gunpowder irritation. I felt that I must present as dreadful an appearance, but I was younger than they were, and nothing can feel as superior as youth.

So I nodded and left them, and walked toward the house, approaching it from the back, where the herb garden was. Levi must have been watching and waiting for me. My own sight was blurred, for the sun was already low and burning into my eyes, and I heard him before I saw him. Shouting, "Adam! Adam! Adam!" he hurtled toward me and plunged into my arms, and I just let my gun drop and hugged him as if he was everything in the world. He was crying, and I began to cry too. I sat down on the ground, still holding him tight, and did my best to stop my tears. I knew that it would be only moments before I had to face Mother, and I didn't want it to be with tears in my eyes. I could imagine that there had been tears enough for that day.

"We thought you were dead," Levi sobbed. "There was a big damn fool from Concord come by here before, and he said he saw you lying dead up at the crossroads."

"Do I look dead?"

"Oh, Adam—I don't want you dead."

"Well, I'm not dead. I'm alive. I may be tired to death, but I'm alive."

"I don't want you dead, Adam."

"Stop saying that I'm dead, because I'm not dead." I shook him, and he looked up at me and managed to smile through his tears. Then I got to my feet, and there, at the edge of the herb garden, Mother was standing with Granny next to her, Granny's arm around her to hold her up, and Mother's face as white as snow. Her mouth was open a little, the lips trembling. Granny just stared at me, shaking her head slightly.

"He's not dead," Levi said apologetically.

Mother took a few steps toward me.

"I'm awful dirty," I whispered. "I guess I never been so dirty in my whole life."

Then Mother came up to me and took me in her arms, holding me so tight I thought my ribs would break, her face buried in my dirty shirt. Then she let go of me and stepped back and began to cry. Granny went over to her, stroking her shoulder and whispering, "Poor dear, poor dear." It seemed to me that Granny might have spared a moment for greeting me, but she hardly appeared to know that I was there. Levi picked up my gun, and Granny led Mother back into the house, myself following them.

A number of neighbors were in the kitchen or standing outside. Ruth was there, and her mother and her widow aunt Susan, and old Mrs. Cartwright, the midwife, who always helps out on funeral occasions, when it comes to the laying out and the shrouding, and there were some of Levi's friends, the Albright boys, and little Jonah Parker, who had death in his own family. They made way for me to enter the kitchen. Ruth held back, but never took her eyes off me, and the Widow Susan took my arm. Mother dropped into a chair and stared at me, her whole body shivering and the tears running down her cheeks, and Granny's face was all twisted up with her own attempt to refrain from weeping realizing, perhaps, that it would only take a little more to have all those women half-hysterical.

I had anticipated a bad time of coming home, but I hadn't thought it would be anywhere as heartbreaking and uncomfortable as this. For the life of me, I didn't know what to say, except to tell Goody Simmons that Cousin Simmons was back and at their house.

"You go there, Ruthie," she told her daughter, "and tell him we're here."

"Shall I take him upstairs?" Mrs. Cartwright asked Mother.

Mother didn't respond, but the Widow Susan nodded, and Mrs. Cartwright took my hand and led me up the stairs and into the main bedroom, where Father's body was laid out on the bed.

At first, I was frightened to death and would have given ten years of my life not to have to go into that room. I held back at the doorway. Mrs. Cartwright cooed at me, "Come, come, now. Nothing to be afraid of. It's birth, marriage, and death. Always has been that way and always will. Some day your own children will look at you all stretched out and washed and combed, and how do you suppose they're going to feel? Now come right in here, Adam."

It was poor consolation, but at least it turned my mind from my fear and reluctance to an old, established, and ever-increasing dislike of Mrs. Cartwright. I was able to assure myself that she was unquestionably the most repulsive and insensitive old lady in Middlesex County, and that was some small comfort. I walked into the room and looked down at Father.

"Pay your respects," she cackled.

"Oh, get out of here and leave me alone, Mrs. Cartwright!" I snapped at her.

"What? Well, I do declare," she began, and I interrupted her and told her in no uncertain terms to get out. Then she left, muttering and coughing with indignation.

I was left alone then with my father, who was not my father but a body, with all that was meaningful and important gone out of it. It was the ending of a day when I had seen many bodies, bodies of redcoats and bodies of Committeemen. All my life long, death had only touched me lightly, but I had lived all day with death today. I was too numb to be moved any more. I didn't even want to weep. Later and many times afterward, I would remember my father, but not the corpse on the bed.

I left the room then, closing the door gently behind me.

When I returned to the kitchen, Mother had composed herself, and Granny came over to me, took my hand, and squeezed it. All the other women had gone. I guess the Simmons women went to greet Cousin Joseph; even though he hadn't been killed, he deserved at least an acknowledgment of his return. Mrs. Cartwright must have stalked out in anger. Levi stood in a corner. He couldn't take his eyes off me.

"You must be hungry," Mother said.

"I am, but I'm dirtier than I'm hungry. I just don't believe I'm home without you remarking on it, Mother."

"I guess it could suffer to be remarked on," Mother nodded, looking at me now the way she would normally regard her son, and not the way you look at someone returned from the dead. "I have seen you dirty before, Adam Cooper, but not this dirty. That's your new coat, isn't it?"

"It is. That's right, Mother."

"How did you tear your shirt that way?" Granny asked me.

"Crawling on my belly through a windfall."

"Indians have bellies," Granny said, fighting her own battle with her own torment, and fighting it gallantly, "but in our family people have had stomachs for as many generations as we care to contemplate."

"Yes, ma'am," I nodded. "I would have said stomach. It was the excitement."

"What excitement? As far as I know, the excitement is over. Where is the redcoat army?"

"Back in Boston, the way I hear it."

There was a momentary, passing glitter in Granny's old eyes, and then civilization reasserted itself. "Back in Boston, you say?"

"Where we drove them. We drove them out—every foot of the way, and all the way back to Boston."

"How many did you kill, Adam?" Levi cried.

"As for you," Mother said to Levi, "there's more important things than shouting gibberish like a heathen. Take a pail and bring more water in here. Your brother's going to wash."

Levi nodded, grabbed a pail, and ran out. I felt sorry for him. Not only did he have to bear the death of Father, which would weigh more heavily upon him than on me, but he must have experienced his first day of taking the kind of tongue-lashing that I considered a normal part of my existence.

"I want no talk of killing in this house," Mother said to me. "The Committee will do what has to be done, and I am ready to accept that. But I will not have people in my home talking as if we had shed the last vestige of our Christianity and become barbarians. If the redcoats were defeated, it was because God willed their defeat and because the awful hand of Jehovah smote them—not because you and others were out there behaving as if you had never known the shelter of a decent Christian home. I will have no boasting and bragging over the death of any human being, whether our people or their people, and I will thank you to remember that, Adam Cooper."

It relieved me enormously to hear Mother talk that way in just that tone. It meant that she was becoming her old self again, that she would pull herself out of her grief, and that our home would be more than I had hoped for. As for the hand of Jehovah, that was not anything to provoke an argument about—especially since the Reverend was bound to support her. For my part, I was so weary and confused at this point, and my recollection of the day was so chaotic, that I was willing to give credit due to anything that had helped us through it.

"Take off your coat," Mother said. Granny, meanwhile, put wood in the hearth and filled another kettle with water. Mother stared at my shirt helplessly and asked Granny:

"Is it worth trying to mend it?"

"Shirts don't grow on trees, Sarah," Granny replied. "We'll wash it and then we'll see. You can't judge a garment when it's dirty." Then she said to me, "There's water heating. Get out of your clothes, boy, and scrub down. Levi will bring you your things."

I stood in the wooden body tub in the kitchen, and soaped myself and scrubbed myself, while Levi brought me water and worked the scrubbing brush on my back. I had a long scratch against my ribs, and Levi wanted to know whether that was where a redcoat musket ball had nicked me.

"That's a real foolish question."

"Well, it's a wound, isn't it?"

"Of course it isn't a wound. It's a scratch I got crawling through the underbrush."

"It seems to me," Levi said, "that if I had been fighting all day in a battle, I would have gotten myself a wound at least."

"Just don't let Mother hear you talking like that," I warned him.

"What's wrong with her, Adam?"

"Who?"

"Mother."

"Well, how would you feel if you were married, with children and everything, and your husband was lying upstairs dead the way Father is?"

He began to blubber. I told him, as kindly as I could, "Now listen to me, Levi. Father's dead. That's all there is to it, and you might as well be a man enough to face it. You can't break into tears every time anyone mentions his name. We have very large responsibilities, you and me."

"What kind of responsibilities, Adam?"

"Well, just every kind. Who's going to take care of Mother and Granny, if we don't? And what about the garden and the farming work? I know that we have some shares in some of the enterprises in Boston, but no one knows if there'll be any income out of that now. You know how Mother is. She wouldn't accept help, because help would be the same as charity, which is all right if you offer it to someone else."

Levi nodded somberly.

"Bring me the towels."

He brought me the towels, and I rubbed myself dry.

"Did you go up and look at Father?" he asked me.

"I did. I went up there with old Mrs. Cartwright."

"I hate her."

176

"I don't like her. But I guess she tries to do the best that she can."

"They say she cuts open dead people and takes out their innards."

"All the fool things you hear!" He handed me the clean clothes and I began to dress. "She's just an old lady."

"She's a witch!"

"You just don't say anything like that. You ought to have better sense."

"What is it like to be dead, Adam?"

"How do I know? I never been dead."

"You don't have to scream at me."

"I'm not screaming at you. But what do you want me to do when you ask all these crazy questions? How do I know what it's like to be dead? I don't know."

"I only mean," Levi protested, "that if you go to heaven, you're not here, are you? I mean Father's not upstairs there on the bed. It's just a body, isn't it?"

"What's the use of talking about that, Levi?"

"I was just thinking about ghosts."

"I don't believe in ghosts," I said. "There's no such thing."

"Jonathan Crisp saw a ghost and talked to it. It was last December."

"He was lying."

"Well, how do you know? How can you say that he was lying, and be so sure about it? You weren't there when he saw the ghost."

"All right. Believe whatever you want. Leave me alone."

"I can't help it."

"What can't you help?" I asked shortly.

"Being afraid."

"Whatever is there to be afraid of now? The redcoats are gone."

"Well, weren't you afraid? Didn't you run away?"

"So did everyone else run away. It's all right for you to talk, but you don't know what it is to stand there and have all those guns go off in your face."

"I would have run away," Levi agreed.

"Well, I'm pleased that you have enough modesty to admit it. I thought maybe that you were braver than the entire Committee."

"Suppose the redcoats come back, Adam?"

"They won't come back. It was a battle, and we won the battle."

"They came back here," Levi said. "A lot of them were bleeding and dead. They carried the dead men. I saw a man whose hand was shot off, and they wrapped his hand in a jacket. He kept on screaming anyway. Saul Parker said he was sure to die. The whole common was filled with them, and they were mighty provoked. You should have heard the way they talked. They broke into the Fairfax place and took all the silver. Then they broke into Joshua Bond's shop and stole everything there, and they set his house on fire, and they set the Loring house on fire too, and Goody Mullikan's house. You never saw anything burn like that, Adam. One of them kicked Goody Fairfax, but then another one of them got mad and said that she was just an old lady, and what did they want to kick her for? Two of them searched our whole house, and Granny followed them from room to room, and she told them that if she were a man, they wouldn't come walking into our house like that. Then they cut the bell ropes in the meetinghouse. They took Mother's silver teapot. She never said a word. Granny ran after them, calling them thieves and cutthroats. They said we were all too rich for dirty gillies. What's a gillie, Adam?"

"Some kind of Scot farmer, I think. Did the other army come here too?"

"They came from Boston. You never saw so many redcoats as were here then. The whole town swarmed with them, and you could hear the shooting from the battle to the east. Did you shoot any of them, Adam—really?"

"I don't know."

"Then they stole all the carriages. They took both our horses—"

"No, they didn't!" I cried.

"They did. They stole the Loring horses and Mr. Bedford's team of grays and all the horses in the livery stables, and the Hancock carriage and the Hodley carriage and both carriages from Buckman's place and all the horses from there—why, they were running around just like they were crazy—and one of them hit me on my head with his crop, feel it, right here."

He pushed his hair aside, and I felt the lump on his head, and asked him, "What did he want to do that for?"

"He said I had no business snooping around, and he cussed me out. One of them threatened to stick his bayonet into Johnny Carver. He's only nine years old. Can you imagine? All we were doing was looking at the dead redcoats. They laid them out on the common—forty-two of them. Then they piled the bodies into the Loring freight wagon and into the other wagons, but you can still see all the bloodstains on the grass on the common. Then they marched out on the Menotomy Road, and they were hardly gone when

the Concord and Sudbury men got here. There
was such yelling and screaming and cheering, and
all the women came running out—with just everybody kissing and hugging, you never saw such a
thing, Adam. Really. Never. Then we thought
we'd ring the bells, but the ropes were cut. Then
I ran home, and Ephraim Colin, who has the mill
outside of Concord, he said he saw you laying
dead. But where were you then, Adam?"

"I was in the big old windfall down on the
Menotomy Road."

"That was a funny place to be."

"It was," I agreed.

While I bathed and dressed in clean clothes,
the neighbors had been coming into the front
room. A number of the women would have come
earlier, but they were waiting for bread to raise
or for pudding to finish, because you can't come
empty-handed to a home of the dead. Others
brought meat roasts, sweetmeats and maple-sugar
crowns, until the dining-room table was loaded
with enough food to last us a month. The women felt that they had to do a certain amount
of weeping just out of respect, and since these
things are contagious, Mother was crying again.
I went over to her, and she took my hands and
said:

"Adam, Adam—whatever are we going to do?"

I tried to tell her that everything would be
all right, and that we would get along. It was
worse for Levi. All the women were overwrought
and distracted after the night and the day they
had lived through, and they had to embrace Levi
and cry over him to their satisfaction. But at
least there was a wonderful closeness, the storm

having swept over all of us, and I think that was a comfort to Mother.

Cousin Simmons and the undertaker and the Fairview brothers, who were a sort of kin to us but distantly, came down the stairs, carrying the coffin; and Cousin Simmons suggested that I help them bear it over to the meetinghouse. I welcomed a reason to take me out of the house and away from the women, for the tears started all over again when they saw the coffin.

We cut across the common with the coffin. It was twilight now, the sun set, and the gentle pink light of evening lying low on the western sky, the color so pretty that it broke my heart to look at it, the air sweet and clean. This was the same place I had fled from twelve hours or so before, but the count of time had no meaning; and the April morning when I had departed properly belonged in a past so distant and different that it could hardly be evoked. Even if all the scars were healed, nothing would ever be the same again.

It was quiet on the common. The blackened ruins of the burned houses still smoked, but there was no sound of war in the air, no smell of gunpowder, no agonized screaming of the wounded, no curses of the enraged.

A cannon, spiked and dismounted, lay on the common, a British supply cart with a broken wheel, and a dozen or so smashed hogsheads. There were broken muskets, bent bayonets, powder bottles, knapsacks. A red uniform coat, torn and bloodstained. A lady's dress and a pewter pot, dropped by a looter. Caleb Harrington's terrier, dead, as if fate tirelessly stalked the Harrington family. A cocked hat, with the ugly mash of skin and blood inside it. No one touched such things; tomorrow, they would be burned. A half a dozen books, with pages torn out and fluttering in the evening breeze, as if there could be no barbarism without the destruction of a book. A child's bonnet—and a shoe. A strange, woeful, pointless litter, where a battle or a massacre had occurred, however it would be recalled and remembered.

I had survived it, but my father and other men had died here, and then the same army that killed my father had been driven back here, hurt and bleeding, to make a rendezvous with a relief army out of Boston. And while they swarmed all over this place, my brother Levi, and the other children of the village, ran among them with that incredible immunity of childhood. For myself, I had parted with childhood and boyhood forever.

"Don't you hear me, Adam?" the undertaker was asking me.

"Yes, sir—I heard you."

"I mean that a man has some feeling about his profession. It's not just an ordinary profession. I like to think that the bereaved take comfort out of my work, but this isn't the best. Hardly. It's makeshift, that's what it is, Adam. The same kind of makeshift that I had to put together for the Parkers and the Hodleys and the Harringtons —and old Mrs. Fess, whose heart gave out. You wouldn't think so, would you, with all this fuss and calamity, and with Archie Hoggins from Watertown—they got dead of their own, believe me —begging for help, well, you just wouldn't think that an old lady would die at a time like this. I offer apologies. It's pine boards knocked together, and not even stained."

"It's all right."

"That's kind of you to say so, Adam. But your

father liked the best. That was one thing you could say about Moses Cooper, he liked the best. The best quality. Now there's no reason why we can't change it later, but—"

I was pleading silently for him to shut up, and I was grateful to Cousin Simmons when he said, "Later is plenty of time for such things. Leave the boy in peace now."

"I didn't mean to trouble the boy, Joseph. I just figured to tell—"

"Leave him in peace. You and I will talk about it if it needs talking about."

When we came to the church, there was quite a small crowd standing around outside, among them a number of people whose faces I didn't recognize. I learned later that all the Committee in Middlesex had appointed representatives to obtain accurate depositions of what had happened on the common, and while there were certainly good intentions at work, I doubt that the clear and absolute truth will ever be known. Inside the meetinghouse were more people, at least half of the Committee, and a good many relatives of the deceased. We laid Father's coffin down next to the coffins that were already in front of the pulpit. It was quite dark now, and Hiram, the sexton, was lighting candles. The Reverend spread a black cloth over Father's coffin, an act which comforted me, for in all truth I had been depressed by the green-pine look of it.

A man who said he was from the *Advertiser*, in Boston, buttonholed me, and asked whether he could question me about what had happened on the common. I was past being able to think clearly, and I begged him to put his questions to someone else.

"Don't you have an interest in the truth, Mr.

Cooper?" He called me mister, anticipating that I wouldn't be able to resist the flattery.

"I'm too tired to know what the truth is."

"A patriot always knows what the truth is."

I stared at him dumbly, a big, bluff man in his forties, dressed in good black worsted and white linen, a broad, fleshy face, a deep, rumbling voice that made my own sound to me like a hopeless squeak. I shook my head and pushed past him out of the church.

The crowd outside in front was larger, and a man who appeared to know just about all there was to know was telling about the situation in Boston—that a siege of the city and the redcoats within it was being planned, and what the pledges of this Committee and that Committee were. I listened to him for a minute or two, and found myself dozing. Then someone took my arm and drew me away.

It was Cousin Simmons. "Come away from there, Adam, my boy," he said. "After a day like ours, it is as hard to endure oratory as the measles. I wish that Moses Cooper was here. He had a most marvelous gift for putting a man in his place."

I nodded, and Cousin Simmons went on, "Don't you think that it is cruel or insensitive of me, Adam, to talk about your father. But it seems to me that it is most harmful for a person to bury the dead in his own heart as well as in the cold earth. Goody Simmons would have the skin off my back were I to cast one small doubt on this question of personal survival after death, and if the truth be told, I know no more than the next one. But I do know that something important survives in our children. Your father was a hard man to know, Adam, and sometimes a body just had to grind his teeth and say, Well, that's Moses Cooper, and that's the way he is, and there isn't one blessed thing you can do to change him. But the way he was, Adam, was a most remarkable way. He was an educated man, like most of the men in our family. He was a prudent man. He put away for a rainy day, and you and your mother will be provided for, but he was not a miserly man. No, sir, he was not. He was a man of many strong convictions, and you had to suffer somewhat to be his friend—or his son."

"I'm not complaining," I muttered.

"I know you are not. Nevertheless, if you recollect him as a saint, you will lose him. Moses Cooper was no saint. He was just as stubborn as a Methodist preacher, but he was a brave man with fine convictions, and I don't think there was ever a day went by that I didn't feel pride and satisfaction in knowing he was my friend."

"Is that true, Cousin Simmons?" I asked him.

"As true as the gospel."

"I was so happy last night," I whispered. "When we walked across to the common, he put his arm on my shoulders. I felt that he truly loved me. That was the first time I ever felt it." My voice broke, and in another moment I would have been crying; but Cousin Simmons put his own big hand on my shoulder, and with the other indicated the houses around the common.

"There it is, Adam."

"Sir?"

"We took up arms for our home place, and he died for it. That's an old, old way, Adam, older than you or me, remember. There are worse ways for a man to die, I tell you."

I nodded. In silence, we walked along the edge of the common, the first of the evening dropping like a curtain all around us; and then Cousin Simmons pointed toward Buckman's Tavern.

"The Committee board meets there tonight, Adam."

"Oh?"

"It was our feeling that we should issue some sort of a statement in regard to and respect for our dead. Some small tribute, which the Reverend could read from the pulpit tomorrow. I think the Committee must be heard on that. Don't you?"

"I do," I agreed. "Father would have been the first to want that for someone else. He was very strong for the Committee."

"Rightly so, Adam. God help us, today was strange enough, but can you imagine what today would have been without the Committees?"

"I think so—yes."

We walked a little farther, and Cousin Simmons said, "They'll be opening the muster book, Adam."

"Sir?"

"It's the word on the siege of Boston. They'll want five thousand Committeemen at least. Every town."

"Will you be signing it, Cousin Simmons?"

"I don't know," he replied slowly. "This is one time I do wish to heaven that I had Moses Cooper's advice. I don't know what's beginning, Adam, or how and when it is going to end. I have three womenfolk at home, no sons, and a forge. A blacksmith's prime to a town, if you ever thought about it, Adam. No smith, no iron. No iron, and the town is going to dry up and die. So I got to consider it. I can't make any snap decisions, can I?"

"No, sir. I don't think you can."

"Any more than you can, Adam."

"Sir?"

"A war has begun, Adam. Not just a battle. But a war. Haven't you thought about that?"

My heart as heavy as lead, I replied, "No, sir. I don't think I have."

"You have to, you know. Now here we are, almost at Buckman's. You're mighty tired, so go home now, Adam. Think about it. I'll see you in the morning."

I said good night to him, and turned back in the direction of my home.

# The Evening

As I walked across the common in the darkness, my thoughts went back to my first awareness of a difference, a breaking away from the past into a future that became alive, selfshaping, apart—or so it seemed—from our own will. I was also bidding childhood farewell, an action not singular and definitive, but repeated many times until the nostalgia so thins that it is meaningless. But I was not yet at that point.

Because we played our game—the one we loved most—right here on the common, and it was only yesterday, my own yesterday; and up to the time when I became too old for games. I was twelve then. At twelve your hands are hard enough for work, but I do remember two more times, during the three years after that, when I played the game, in spite of my size, my long bones, my flat, strong muscles that could lift a plough off the ground.

We called the game Pontiac. Once, Pontiac had been a villainous red Indian, but by the time I was old enough for the game, he had changed into a hero. We were children who knew little enough of what went on in the talk and minds of our elders, but we knew that Pontiac, who had been bad, who had slaughtered the men of General Braddock, was no longer bad. He became a valid hero, so to say. The game was played this way. However many of us there were, we divided ourselves into two parts. The redcoats made an outside circle. The Indians were inside the circle. The redcoats had a ball, which they flung back and forth across the circle, attempting to hit the Indians. Each Indian hit was eliminated; he had to remove himself from the game, which he usually did after substantial argument —and in time, one Indian was left, a boy who could now avoid the ball easily enough, since he had no one to interfere with or confuse his movements. He was Pontiac, and he had the right to choose any redcoat he pleased for scalping. The scalp was by rule limited to a hank of back hair, no thicker than a small finger; but many a boy with an ugly gap in his back hair had some explaining to do at home. I, myself, was scalped twice, but I had been Pontiac at least a dozen times, and I had the scalps hidden in my room to prove it.

And now, as I walked home across the common, I remembered the game and childhood and clung to both, but hopelessly. By the time I entered my house, I had surrendered them.

The house was filled with neighbors. The widow Susan Simmons had taken charge in the kitchen, and the whole house was warm with the smell of good things cooking and baking. I think that then I was somewhat upset that so much attention should be paid to food and cooking and eating in a house where death had been, but as time goes on I appreciate the deep wisdom of it. Food is close to the meaning of life. There are tributes enough to the dead; the food is a tribute to the living, who are in need of it at the time. There could have been no better consolation for Mother than the need to feed hungry people, among them myself.

"Adam, I told you to eat before, and you never

did," she said to me. "I can't depend on you to take a crust of bread if my back is turned."

That was certainly new, and a part of the difference; formerly, any reference to my stomach likened it to a bottomless pit. She used to say to the neighbors, "I don't know where the boy puts it. I just don't know. But it frightens me to watch what he does to pie or to hot bread." Now, I was going to starve myself if she didn't feed me forcibly. For her, I had to be a man with terrible urgency; there was no time to dream about the games I had played on the common. She had taken a grip on herself, and now when she wept, she would weep out of the sight of others; but she had to tell herself that here was a man, Adam Cooper, fifteen years old, but overnight a man. But I wasn't. It doesn't work that way.

I sat down at the kitchen table, and the women fussed over me and set twice the amount before me than even I could consume. But once I began to eat, I couldn't stop until I was near to bursting with roast and pudding and hot bread and pie. While I ate, the women whispered about me: "Poor boy, he looks so tired." "Such a fine boy." "Such a dependable boy." "I always said so about Adam Cooper, and I was right."

Levi sat opposite me with hero-worshiping eyes. He had brought my fowling piece in from outside where I had dropped it, and cleaned it and polished it until the metal shone like silver. In his mind, too, I had departed from a childhood we once shared. No more battles between us, no more threats or name-calling.

"Now he feels better," one of the women said, with the triumphant satisfaction a woman can exhibit when she sees a man well fed. But I felt no better—only more tired, more hopeless, more defeated.

Ruth was there again, now. She stayed on the other side of the room and looked at me whenever she felt others would not notice. In the candlelight and the firelight, she was lovelier than I remembered. But I wanted to cry out to her, "Too quickly, too quickly! Can't you see what they're doing to me? Don't let them do it to you." But she wanted it. Her eyes were the eyes of a woman, and whatever the future held, she would not be afraid of it.

When I had finished eating, Mother took me aside into the pantry and said to me, "Where is Father lying now?"

"In front of the pulpit with the other coffins. The Reverend covered them with black cloth."

She nodded, and then was silent for a moment.

"Adam?"

"Yes, Mother."

"If I don't appear just the same—I mean the way you think about me as your mother—today and even tomorrow, you understand—"

"I understand," I said.

"I mean that all you went through today, so much —oh, my God, so much, and I can't even talk to you about it, or listen to your story about it. Do you understand?"

"Of course I understand, Mother."

"In a little while—a few days."

"I know, Mother."

"Are you very tired now, Adam?"

"It's funny," I said, "but I was more tired before."

"That's good. I want you to take a package of candles over to the meetinghouse."

"Mother, what for?"

"Take them there. I don't want him to lie in the darkness tonight."

"But, Mother, the Reverend has candles. They're burning now. The place isn't dark."

"Let these candles be for later."

"All right," I agreed. "I'll take them there, Mother."

Granny sat at the kitchen table and made the long, green bayberry candles into a package. She had become an old lady. She had been my grandmother, but until tonight I had not thought of her as an old lady, withered and consumed; and it occurred to me that she had lost more than I lost. Nature rules wisely at times, and it's in the order of things that the parent dies before the child. Granny had lost too much.

"Adam dear," she said to me, "tell the Reverend that if these tapers are lighted, they will burn until the dawn comes. They are extra thick. I never thought it when I dipped them. I never thought it at all." I kissed her cheek, and the women fussed over her.

Before I left, I glanced around for Ruth, but she had gone. I went out through the herb garden, and just outside the gate, Ruth was waiting for me.

"What's that you're carrying, Adam?" she whispered.

"Candles. Mother wants them at the meeting-house, so Father won't lie in the darkness."

Ruth nodded. "Could you lay them down a moment?"

I placed them on the wayfarer's bench, and Ruth flung her arms around me and kissed me again and again. It was like I had never kissed her or embraced her before, her mouth so warm and soft, her body so tightly against me. "Oh, Adam—Adam," she said, "when the news came that you were dead, my whole world died. Every bit of it. Nothing was left. My head was empty and my heart was empty, and I knew that I would grow old like Goody Hartman and become a skinny, dried-up old maid."

I just couldn't see Ruth Simmons as a skinny, dried-up old maid. One of the things we had in common was an appetite, and at the Thanksgiving dinner, November past, the two of us had astounded the family, who declared that our performance was stunning, even for Massachusetts. But I was moved that she should feel that way.

"I love you so much, Adam. I'm not afraid to say it now. I want to."

I guess I returned her feelings, even if I did take it somewhat more for granted. I couldn't think of myself as being married to anyone but Ruth Simmons—if only because there were so many things about myself that she just shrugged away and accepted, things I would have the devil's own time explaining to another girl. I also had a strong suspicion that Ruth would make life unbearable for any other girl I took up with. But such things as marriage had been comfortably in the future.

Ruth knew me well enough to reassure me, and told me that it was all right. "You don't think I want to be married at the age of fifteen?"

I knew that the Simmonses, men and women, were strongminded, and I mentioned that.

"Adam Cooper, how you talk sometimes!"

"You want to walk over to the church with me?"

"Of course I do," she said.

I picked up the candles, and we started toward the common, holding hands and walking very slowly. It was most comforting, and I couldn't help thinking how rewarding and pleasant it would be if we could be together all this night and the next night too. Then I thought of Ruth and the other women too—alone in the town through the length of this day, with the town and the children and everything else as their burden, and the dead men to lay out themselves, never knowing whether their men were alive or dead or would ever return to them. I spoke about it to Ruth, and how hard it must have been.

"It was harder for you, out with the battle," she said.

"I'm not sure. A battle's a funny thing—this one, anyway. It wasn't like any battle I ever read about in books. It was terribly confused. No one seemed to know much about what was going on or what to do, except to shoot at the redcoats."

"Did you, Adam?"

"Know what to do? No. Not a blessed bit."

"I meant, did you shoot at the redcoats?"

"A few times, yes. I only had bird shot in my gun, so mostly they were out of my range."

"Did you kill anyone?" she whispered.

"No. I hit some soldiers once, because I saw them jump and yell out with pain. But I don't think I killed anyone."

"Did you want to, Adam?"

"Maybe once, but only for a little while. I don't hate anyone enough to want to kill him."

"I'm glad you feel that way," Ruth said. "I can't get used to thinking that we have to kill and fight now. I was upstairs at a window this morning when the redcoats fired. I saw one of them drive his bayonet into Jonas Parker's back when he was trying to run away."

"You shouldn't have watched that."

"But they could come back, couldn't they, Adam, and then it could happen all over again?"

I was silent for a while before I replied, "No. It couldn't happen all over again."

"Why not?"

I shook my head.

"Why not, Adam?"

"Because it isn't the same any more," I said finally. "We aren't the same. This morning, we knew that we wouldn't fight. But now we know that we must fight, and we're learning how."

Crossing the common, we met the Reverend, and I told him how I was bringing the candles to the meetinghouse.

"By all means, bring them there and let them be lighted, if that will please your mother, Adam. I have the place lit and intended to keep it so all night; but if it brings her comfort to have more light there—then let it be so. For myself, I am on my way to see your mother now. I have so many calls to make. We are a town of sorrow and tragedy —and it happened too quickly."

"She'll be pleased to see you, sir."

"And Adam?"

"Sir?"

"Do you know about the muster?"

"I know about it, Reverend. My Cousin Simmons told me."

"Well, Adam," the Reverend said slowly, "I am not one of those who might regard you as a boy. You lived a man's life today and you did a man's work. But think about it, Adam. Think about it. Youth is too easily shamed into action. Pride is strong and potent, Adam—but let me only remind you that your first duty is to your mother. She needs you right now as she never needed you before. A week or a month from now, it might be different, but now she needs you, Adam."

I nodded. "I have been thinking about it."

"Good. And if I am not at your home when you return, Adam, God bless you and sleep well. And you too, Ruth."

He left us, and when he was out of earshot, Ruth asked me what he meant.

"How do you mean?"

"He spoke about the muster. What did my father tell you?"

"I suppose you'll know tomorrow anyway. The British army was driven back into Boston, and the Board of Safety made the decision to besiege Boston. So they called a muster of all the Committees and a general mobilization of the militia. Not only here, Ruth, but everywhere in New England the Committees will send their men to fight at Boston."

"And you'll go? Oh, no, Adam—you wouldn't!"

"I didn't say I'd go. Did I say I'd go?"

"You didn't say so—"

"Then why make such a fuss? I'm certainly not going tomorrow or the next day. But I don't know what's going to come, Ruth. I wish I did, but I just don't."

We walked on to the meetinghouse, Ruth saying never a word more until we were there. The meetinghouse was well lighted, and there were still a good many people inside. Ruth hung back. "I don't want to go in there where the coffins are," she whispered.

"You don't have to if you don't want to. But there's nothing to be afraid of. It's my father there and his friends. Is that anything to be afraid of?"

She went inside with me, then. It was very quiet inside the church now. The strangers had gone away, and those who remained were friends and relatives of the dead men. They sat here and there in the pews, mostly men and some boys, some of them with their Bibles open on their laps, but most of them sitting silently. I whispered a greeting to some of them and nodded at others, and then I lit our candles and put them in brackets, leaving half of them for later. Others must have had the same notion as Mother did, for there was a stack of unlit candles on the tract table —to which I added mine.

"I think we should stay for a while," I said softly to Ruth. She nodded. We sat down in our family pew, and after a few minutes, Ruth began to cry. I thought she was entitled to that. I felt that there was no woman in our town who was not entitled to weep her fill after today.

Ruth dried her eyes. I could see that she was more relaxed and that she felt better. She was very tired now, and so was I.

We walked back across the common to the Simmons house, and at the door, Ruth said to me, "Adam, do you love me?"

I thought about it for a while before I answered. I had known Ruth Simmons all my life, and with a girl you know all your life, you are likely to take things for granted. About a year ago, we had been to Boston to visit some of Mother's relatives, and I met a fourth or fifth cousin or something of that sort—a girl of sixteen with blue eyes and long yellow hair. I thought at the time that she was the most beautiful thing I had ever seen in my life, and I fell madly in love with her, even though I never saw her again. My passion for her lasted five or six weeks, and then it kind of dwindled. I had never fallen in love with Ruth in just that way, but then neither had the feeling I had for her dwindled. It remained on a kind of even keel, except for moments like this, when I felt closer to her than to anyone in the world. So after thinking about it, I nodded, and said, Yes, I thought I loved her about as much as I would ever love any girl.

"I love you, Adam Cooper," she told me. "I don't change easily. Even if this war lasts a whole lifetime, it won't change my feelings about you."

"A lifetime's a long while."

"I don't care."

Then I kissed her and bid her good night.

Only the Simmons women still remained with Mother and Granny when I came home, and a short while after I arrived, they left. Levi was sound asleep. Like myself and so many others, he had missed the sleep of the night before. Mother and Granny were both of them exhausted, and I suggested that we all go to bed.

"I won't sleep," Mother said.

"You will, Mother, because you must."

"No, I won't sleep," she said.

Granny took her upstairs. There were things that had to be done at night that Father usually did. I did them, and then I drew water from the well for the morning. Granny was back in the kitchen when I returned.

"Is Mother sleeping?"

"Sound asleep when her head touched the pillow," Granny said.

"And you, Granny?"

"I need little sleep, Adam."

"Then I'll be going along."

"Yes—"

At the door, I paused and said to her, "Granny, I had Father only a while. Sometimes, I feel that I had him, the way you have a father and love him, only last night. You had him a long time."

"He was your father but my child," Granny said softly.

"I love you, Granny. You have me and you have Levi."

"Do I, Adam?"

"Yes."

"Do I, Adam? Do you think the news of the muster isn't all over the town? When will you be going away, Adam Cooper?"

"No one said I was going."

"You may lie to others, Adam. But don't lie to me."

"I'm not lying, Granny," I protested. "I just haven't made up my mind about anything. I'm too tired to think about it anyway."

"But you thought about it?"

"I suppose so, Granny."

"Time will come, you'll go."

"I guess you're right, Granny. A time will come and I'll go. There's no way out of it. But let's not talk about it tonight. Come upstairs with me, Granny."

"No. Go ahead, Adam. I'll sit here a while and think. Plenty to think about, you know."

I went over to her and kissed her and said good night.

In my bed, with the covers drawn up close around me, I closed my eyes and whispered a prayer. Not the same prayer as all the other nights. I said, "Thank you, God, that today is over." Then, falling asleep, I said farewell to a childhood, a world, a secure and sun-warmed existence and past that was over and done with and gone away for all time.